A

OR DEATH?

The Rocky Mountains teem with life. Deer. Elk. A host of smaller animals.

The mountains also teem with predators. Coyotes. Wolves. Cougars. Bears.

The most fearsome of all are grizzlies.

Just ask Nate King. Long known as Grizzly Killer, he has tangled with the great bears more often than most.

Or ask the two families who have come to the mountains to start a new life.

Unknown to all of them, one particular grizzly is on a killing spree.

And their paths are about to cross.

Books by David Robbins

Endworld Universe
ENDWORLD
WILDERNESS
WHITE APACHE   BLOOD FEUD
A GIRL, THE END OF THE WORLD AND EVERYTHING
A GIRL A DOG AND ZOMBIES ON THE MUNCH

Series
ANGEL U
DAVY CROCKETT

Horror
PRANK NIGHT   SPOOK NIGHT
HELL-O-WEEN   THE WERELING
THE WRATH   SPECTRE

Novels
HIT RADIO   BLOOD CULT

Westerns
GUNS ON THE PRAIRIE   THUNDER VALLEY
RIDE TO VALOR   TOWN TAMERS
BADLANDERS   DIABLO
THE RETURN OF THE VIRGINIAN

Movie Novelizations
MEN OF HONOR   PROOF OF LIFE
TWISTED

Nonfiction
HEAVYE TRAFFIC
(A history of the DEA)

WILDERNESS #71

STALKED

by

David Robbins

©2020 by David L. Robbins

All rights reserved. No part of this publication may be reproduced, distributed, transmitted in any form or introduced into a retrieval system, by any means, (electronic, mechanical, photocopying, recording or otherwise) without the prior written permission of the author, except in the case of brief quotations embodied in critical reviews and certain other noncommercial uses permitted by copyright law.

Any such distributions or reproductions of this publication will be punishable under the United States Copyright Act and the Digital Millenium Copyright Act to the fullest extent including Profit Damages (SEC 504 A1), Statutory Damages (SEC 504 2C) and Attorney Fees and Court Costs.

DISCLAIMER: This is a fictional work. Names, characters, places and incidents either are the product of the author's imagination or are used fictitiously and any resemblance to actual persons, living or dead, business establishments, events or locales is entirely coincidental.

Published by Mad Hornet Pub.
Printed in the United States of America
ISBN: 978-1-950096-16-9

Chapter 1

She was eleven years old.

Her name was Clara. She had spent her entire life in South Carolina and then her folks decided to head west.

Mostly it was her pa's notion, and her ma went along with the idea. He went on and on about the Rocky Mountains.

Clara never understood why. She was happy where they were. They were hill folk and had a cozy cabin and forty acres. Their kin were close by, and she had friends she got to see and play with whenever her ma went visiting.

The talk of the Rockies scared her. It would take forever to get there. Wild animals were everywhere, she heard. Bears and wolves and whatnot. And critters called buffalo, whatever they were.

Indians were everywhere, too. Not the friendly kind that Clara knew but hostiles. Indians who liked to kill people. Indians who, or so her uncle claimed, liked to steal little girls and raise them as their own.

Clara had a lot of reasons for not wanting to go. But her pa had made up his mind and her ma told her to hush when she tried to talk them into staying.

Her older brother by four years, Jacob, was keen on

heading west, too. But Jacob was always keen on anything their pa wanted.

Her older sister, Alice, who was sixteen, didn't want to go, either. Since they hardly ever saw eye to eye on things, Clara was tickled pink until she learned the reason Alice didn't want to go was because of a boy who lived over the next hill.

Getting ready was a chore. Their pa bought a wagon, a huge thing with a canvas top. He also bought a team of oxen. They were so big, Clara was wary of going near them.

It didn't help her peace of mind any when her uncle mentioned that buffalo were even bigger.

They spent weeks loading their belongings. Packing and lifting and toting until Clara thought her back and arms would wear out. She didn't complain, though. Nothing brought out her ma's switch faster than sassing her parents, unless it was lying.

Finally they were ready. The wagon was so full, there was barely room for them. Everything was so cramped. When Clara remarked to that effect, her ma said not to let it get to her, that she would be walking alongside the wagon most of the way, anyway.

Clara grew to wish her pa never heard of the Rockies.

She had never minded walking. But to do it from shortly after sunrise until shortly before sunset, day after day after day, it go to be that she hated waking up in the morning because she would endure more trudgery.

Things got a little better when they reached Missouri. There they joined up with other wagons.

Most were bound for something called Oregon Country. Her pa, thank goodness, wasn't going all that way.

Still, the Rocky Mountains were a fair piece, and they had to cross the prairie to get there. Her uncle had told her the prairie was like the ocean, which she saw once, only it was a sea of grass and not water. She thought he was joshing but it turned out he was right.

Unfortunately, if there was anything more boring than a sea of grass, Clara had yet to make its acquaintance.

Grass, grass and more grass for as far as the eye could see. Oh, there were trees and such, but not a lot. Much of the prairie was flatland, or close to.

Clara saw deer on occasion. A couple of mornings she spied elk. Rabbits were common at first but not so many later. The one thing she saw the most of were grasshoppers.

Each day repeated itself. Up early. Hitch the team. A quick meal and off they went. Mile upon mile of walking. A short break in the middle of the day and then more plodding. Toward sundown they would stop and circle the wagons and then the best part of the day commenced. The cooking pots were put on, and they would eat leisurely, and socialize.

Clara liked the socializing. She always did cotton to people. Jacob, not so much. Alice did if they were boys her age.

Still, overall, their journey was as tiresome as could be.

Except at night. The sky was beautiful. Her ma would let her lie out and admire the stars, and lordy, they were grand. There were more than she ever saw back to home.

After an eternity of slogging, one afternoon the scout came galloping back and the wagon master gave the order to halt. There was a lot of excited talk, and the next thing Clara knew, Indians appeared. Not a lot. She counted ten. They stayed off a ways and stared. She couldn't tell much except they wore buckskins with a lot of fringe and were armed with bows and lances. To her surprise, the wagon master and the scout took a cow out to them, and off they went.

The next cause of excitement left her near breathless with wonderment.

Another halt had been called and the wagon master came down the line telling everyone to stay with their wagons and the herd should miss them.

Clara didn't understand the herd part until a rumbling sound from the north grew steadily louder.

Buffalo. Hundreds. Maybe thousands. More than Clara could count. Not that she could see much for the dust, and the fact the buffalo didn't come any nearer than a quarter-mile, or so her pa said. She saw how big they were, though. And she saw lots and lots of horns.

Later word came that it had been a small herd spooked by something or other and running itself out.

Not long after came the moment Clara was dreading.

They came within sight of the Rocky Mountains. Peaks so high, they looked to touch the clouds. Soon foothills appeared, and with them, a parting of the ways.

Most of the wagons broke off to the northwest and

the next leg of their trek to Oregon Country. Half a dozen headed south, making for some place called Bent's Fort, and beyond that, Santa Fe.

Only two wagons continued due west.

Theirs, and one other.

The other family were the Walberg's. They were German. They spoke with an accent that sometimes made Clara giggle. They were nice, though. Their pa, Otto, and her pa got along great. Mrs. Walberg was a plump woman who jiggled all over when she laughed. They had two sons, one not much older than Alice, and a boy who was a year younger than Clara. His name was Gunther. He was painfully shy. Whenever Clara talked to him, he'd blush a lot.

From what Clara was told, the Walberg's originally planned to go all the way to Oregon Country. But her pa's constant talk about how a man could live as he pleased in the Rockies with no one to tell him different had an effect on Otto Walberg. Otto decided nothing would do but his family should live the same as theirs.

Clara's ma was pleased. Clara overheard her telling Alice that she had never liked the notion of them striking off alone, and to have another family for neighbors would be a great relief.

Their last evening with the wagon train, as they were sitting around the fire with the Walberg's, the scout came up and said right out, "What's this I hear about you striking off on your own?"

Clara never liked the scout much. He was a small man with a scar on the left side of his face that was hard for her to look at. It made her queasy. Folks said he got the scar in a fight with Indians. He never went anywhere without his rifle and a brace of pistols and a big bone-handled knife.

Her pa lowered his coffee cup and nodded. "That we are. Mr. Walberg and me."

The scout placed the stock of his rifle on the ground and wrapped his hands around the barrel. "You reckon that's smart?"

"Here now," her pa said. "I won't be insulted."

The scout looked at Clara's ma and Mrs. Walberg and then at each of the children, and shook his head. "I'd just hate to hear that anything happened to your families, is all."

"We can take care of ourselves," her pa said.

"Lot of folks think that." The scout turned and gazed toward the night-shrouded mountains. "Listen. I'll say my piece so my conscience is clear. Then it's on your shoulders." Before her pa could respond, the scout went on. "Those mountains are like nothing you've ever known. Like nothing you've ever heard of. You probably figure you can handle a few hostiles but there's a heap more than a few. And they won't be your worst problems."

Her pa glanced at her ma and Mrs. Walberg. "I don't want you scaring our womenfolk."

The scout stepped closer to her pa and his voice hardened. "Pay heed, mister. There are bears up there that can rip you to pieces with one blow. There are painters and wolves and rattlers. The weather itself will try to do you in. Winters are fierce cold. Summers are godawful dry."

"That's enough," her pa said.

"Not hardly. I can count on less than ten fingers the

number of folks who have gone up there and made a go of it. Settlers, I mean. Not men like Nate King and Shakespeare McNair, who live as far in as anyone...."

Her pa interrupted with, "If they can do it so can we."

"You're not them. They were two of the first. Got their start as trappers. Well, King did. McNair is as old as Methuselah. They live off the land as good as any Injun. And better than you can ever hope to."

Her pa glared.

The scout let out with a loud sigh. "All right. I'm done. Except for this." He paused. "Stick together. Settle close. Find a valley with good grass and plenty of game. If Injuns come around be as friendly as you can be lessen they let fly with arrows or try to slit your throat. Invite them to supper or give them a geegaw. And remember this." He raised his right hand about neck high and held his first two fingers pointing straight up, then raised his hand as high as his head.

"What in the world was that?" her pa said.

"Sign language," the scout said. "That means 'friend'."

Mr. Walberg said, "I have heard Indians use many such signs, yes?"

"They do," the scout confirmed. "You ever get a chance to learn them, do so." He hefted his rifle and turned to go.

"Thank you for your advice," Mr. Walberg said.

The scout nodded, then once again looked at Clara's ma and Mrs. Walberg. "Take care, ladies."

Clara was startled when, quite unexpectedly, the scout stepped over to her and Alice. "Did you see the sign I made?"

"I did," Alice said.

Clara nodded.

"Practice it," the scout said. "Always stay alert when you're out and about. Keep looking behind you. If you come on a bear or a painter, don't run if there's no need. Running will sometimes provoke them. Climbing a tree might save you from a bear but it won't help against the big cats. They can climb better than you." He smiled and wheeled and departed."

"What was that all about?" Clara found her voice.

"Advice," Alice said. "He wants us to live."

"Him and me, both," Clara said.

Chapter 2

Her pa was loco. Her ma came right out and said it in front of everybody.

It was ten days after they broke away from the other wagons. Ten days of wending in among the foothills.

At first the going was easy enough. The gaps between the hills were mostly flat. The oxen plodded along at their usual snail's pace. But then they got to where the land began to climb. In spots it rose steeply and they had to goad the teams on, which became a chore in itself.

By the tenth day the highest foothill yet loomed before them as if to bar their way. To go up it was impossible. Their wagon was too big, too heavy. They'd have to toss half of their belongings out, and even then there was no guarantee the oxen could make it.

The common sense thing to do was go around. But Clara's pa insisted on trying to find a way over. Which was when her ma paused with her soup soon half to her mouth and called him loco.

The Walberg's were unusually quiet. Mr. Walberg, in particular, wasn't his usual cheerful self. Several times that afternoon Clara saw him gaze at the mountain and shake his head and mutter.

Now he coughed and spoke.

"I am thinking, friend Charles, that we have made a mistake. Our hopes got the better of our judgement." Walberg gestured toward the mountain. "Our wagons are sturdy and have brought us many miles but they do not have wings. To attempt the impossible would be foolish. And dangerous."

"There must be a way," her pa declared.

"What if there isn't? What if we break down? What if we end up stranded? Here in the wilderness with our families?" Mr. Walberg shook his head. "I am not willing to put those I care for at such risk."

"Don't give up yet," her pa said. "Let's go a little further."

Mr. Walberg looked at his wife and children. "I am sorry. Tomorrow I turn around. Perhaps if we hurry we can overtake the other wagons....."

"You'd really give up? So soon?"

Walberg fingered his tin cup and took a sip of his coffee. "I liked your idea. I truly did. But I did not expect the going to become so difficult."

They went on talking. Clara's pa was doing his utmost to persuade Walberg to keep going. The women said little. They didn't have to. Their faces told Clara that they agreed with Mr. Walberg. Even her own ma.

Clara lost interest and turned away from the fire. Frankly, she didn't care what they did. She never wanted to leave South Carolina.

Clara was seated on a log between Alice and Jacob, both of whom were intent on the argument. She stared up at the stars and off toward the black peaks and then at the forest that came within a stone's throw of their camp, and her breath caught in her throat.

A pair of eyes were staring back at her.

Big eyes.

Eyes that didn't blink.

Eyes that seemed to be glowing.

Clara figured that was because of their campfires. She had seen eyeshine before. Deer and the like. But not eyes like these.

Fear rippled down her spine. She realized that whatever it was, the thing was huge. The size of the eyes and how far apart they were told her that.

Clara tried to speak, to let everyone else know, but she couldn't get the words out. She was frozen in place. She tried to swallow, to wet her throat so she could yell, but her mouth was bone dry.

Then the eyes came toward her.

Slowly.

Oh-so-slowly.

No one else noticed. Not any of the adults. Not her sister or brother.

Clara wanted to crawl into her own skin and hide. She clenched her fists until her fingernails bit into her palms. It didn't help. She still couldn't speak.

The owner of those awful eyes came to the edge of trees.

Clara saw it. Framed between a pair of oaks. She saw the great oval of the head and the broad brow and its two rounded ears high on top. She saw the whitish snout and a black nose.

It was a bear. Similar to the black bears she had caught sight of back to home now and then. Only this bear was bigger. A lot bigger. And chocolate brown instead of black.

She knew then what it was.

All the talk about them on the long trek across the plains. The scourge of the Rockies, folks said. The lords of creation, said others. Monsters, everyone agreed.

Grizzly bears.

A sharp tingle shot through her and Clara jumped to her feet and screamed.

"What in tarnation?" Jacob blurted, and he jumped up, too.

Alice recoiled, glanced in the direction Clara was gaping, and let out a cry of her own.

Suddenly everyone was yelling or screaming or cursing.

Clara's pa was running toward their wagon where he had leaned his rifle.

Mr. Walberg was bellowing to, "Back away! Back away!"

Mrs. Walberg shrieked fit to burst eardrums.

Jacob spun and raced to fetch his own gun.

In all the confusion hardly anyone except Clara noticed that the grizzly bear was gone. One instant it was there, the next it wasn't. Almost as if it had vanished into thin air.

Clara found her voice. "Look!" she shouted. "Look!" Trying to make everyone realize the bear wasn't there anymore.

"Where? Where?" her pa yelled. He and Jacob and Mr. Walberg's oldest boy, Hermann, dashed over to the forest with their rifles to their shoulders.

Only there was nothing to shoot.

"It's gone!" Clara hollered.

They all looked at one another and at the woods Mrs. Walberg gave a nervous laugh.

"*Danke Gott!*"

Clara didn't know what that meant. She was so relieved, she clapped and squealed in delight.

"Is it really?" her ma said.

"A grizzly, by God!" her pa said. "Came right up and looked us in the eye!" He laughed as if it were a great joke.

Clara didn't think it was funny at all. Judging by the size of its head, the thing was twice as big as any black bear, maybe bigger. "What if it comes back?" she gave voice to her innermost fear.

"It won't!" her pa said. "We scared it off, like we would most any other."

"I am not so sure, my friend," Mr. Walberg said. "Grizzlies are not the same as the bears you are used to in South Carolina."

"How would you know?" her pa said. "You're from Pennsylvania, wasn't it? From Philadelphia?"

"Germantown, yes," Mr. Walberg said.

"Where there aren't any bears at all," her pa said.

"I have heard stories," Mr. Walberg insisted. "You heard them too. From our friends with the wagon train."

"Spook talk is all that was," her pa said. "People love to tell scary stories."

"That grizzly was scary," Clara made bold to say. Her ma told her to hush and beckoned her over.

"Don't sass, girl. You know we don't like that."

Everyone was so excited, they stayed up late talking.

STALKED

Clara didn't take part. She was upset. Powerful upset. Her pa never took anything she said seriously. And her ma was always carping about her talking back when all she was really doing was saying how she felt.

Her elbows in her lap and her chin in her hands, Clara stared at the black woods and swore she could feel the grizzly staring back. She didn't see it, though. She imagined it waiting until they turned in and then stalking out of the forest to devour them in their sleep. "I hate this," she said to herself.

"What was that?" Alice said.

"Nothing."

"I heard you," Alice said.

"I was talking to myself," Clara said. "Let it be."

"Ma's right," Alice said. "You're too sassy for your own good."

The remark didn't improve Clara's mood any. She sat and sulked and was glad when her pa announced it was time for everyone else to turn in. He was going to sit up a while and keep watch.

Clara liked to sleep under their wagon instead of in it because inside was so cramped. Tonight she put up with it. She climbed in and curled up close to the canvas at the rear. She didn't look at the others as they climbed in. Pulling her blanket up over her head, she closed her eyes and waited to drift off.

Jacob fell asleep quick enough. She heard his heavy breathing. So did Alice. Her ma took longer, and shifted and tossed a lot.

Finally only Clara was awake. She eased onto her back and stared at the canvas top and tried not to fidget. When she couldn't take it anymore, she crept to the gate and eased over it and dropped lightly to the ground.

The fire had burned low. Her pa was beside it, his chin on his chest, sound asleep. His rifle was between his legs, the barrel propped on his shoulder.

Clara went to wake him but stopped. He could use the sleep. Instead, she tiptoed over and hunkered next to him. Since she wasn't sleepy, she could keep watch a spell and wake him when her own eyes became heavy.

The forest was a wall of ink, only a few boles and branches visible.

Clara quietly added a piece of tree limb from the pile her brother and Hermann had collected to the fire. The flames grew and she added another. She could see more of the woods, which reassured her.

The stars were a wonderment. So many, so bright. She never tired of the spectacle. Back to home, she would often lay and stargaze until close to midnight. But it was never as grand as this.

She looked for the moon but it was nowhere to be seen. Which was a shame. The last full moon, out on the prairie, was a sight to behold. So big and bright, she swore she could reach out and touch it.

Clara grinned at the memory and closed her eyes and yawned. When she opened them again, the big eyes in the forest were staring back at her.

Clara gasped. She blinked, thinking maybe she was imagining things, but no, the eyes were there, all right.

The grizzly had come back.

Clara swallowed and her knees grew weak. She should wake her pa but once again she was frozen in place. Her fear was so strong, she thought she would wet herself.

The eyes blinked.

Clara turned and gripped her pa's sleeve and gave him a hard shake, whispering, "Pa! Pa! The grizzly!"

He came awake in a befuddled state, glancing every which way and saying, "What? What was that?"

"The grizzly!" Clara repeated, and pointed.

Only it wasn't there.

"Eh?" Her pa stood and swung his rifle left and right and back again. "Where, girl?"

"I thought for sure it was there," Clara said uncertainly.

Her pa frowned and for a moment she thought he was going to give her a piece of his mind. Instead, he wearily smiled and said, "What are you doing up, anyhow? Climb back in the wagon and get to sleep. Don't worry. I won't let anything happen to you. Not ever." He bent and pecked her on the head.

"Yes, pa," Clara said. She did as he told her. But as she lay in the wagon with her blanket over her head, the one thing she couldn't do was stop worrying.

Chapter 3

The next morning Clara wasn't finished her breakfast when her pa went up to Mr. Walberg and placed his hand on Walberg's shoulder.

"Please don't leave, Otto. Give it another day or two. If we don't find a way up then the both of us will head after the wagon train. I had my heart set on living in the Rockies but Oregon Country might suit just as well."

Mr. Walberg and Hermann were in the act of hitching their team. Walberg frowned and looked at his wife.

"Another day or two won't hurt," she said---but she didn't seem pleased. "And after coming all this way, why not?"

"*Wie du liebes wunschst*," Mr. Walberg said. He didn't appear pleased either.

"Thank you!" Clara's pa said. He was so relieved, he clasped Walberg in a hug. Walberg turned red in the face.

"Two more days, then," her pa said, and beamed at her ma.

The sun was barely above the eastern rim of the world when they started out.

As usual, Clara walked beside their wagon. She

hadn't gotten much sleep and she was tired. Her head down, she kicked at small rocks now and then.

She missed South Carolina so much, she was fit to cry.

They traveled a mile or more when she realized someone was beside her and felt a prick on her arm.

"Morning," Gunther said.

Clara was taken aback. Gunther always stayed close to his family's schooner. She was the one who had to go to him to talk. This was a first.

"What do you think?" Gunther said.

"Of going on? I don't have a say. It's up to my pa. Big decisions are always up to him and ma. Me, I have to do as they want or have a switch taken to my backside."

"They hit you?"

"Not in a long time, no," Clara admitted. "But ma does every now and again when I act up, as she calls it.".

"Ah." Gunther gazed at the nearby forest. "I meant the bear."

"What is there to think?" Clara said. "It was there and it was gone. I'm just glad it left us be."

"There will be more like it," Gunther said. "My father says there are many of those grizzlies in these mountains."

"I've heard they're pretty common out here, yes," Clara said.

Gunther glanced over his shoulder, then said quietly, "My *mutter* is very worried."

"Your what? Oh. Your mother? Why did she agree to go on then?"

"She feels bad about leaving all of you. My *vater* too

but he says it is best."

"*Vater?*"

"Sorry," Gunther said. "My father. I heard him and my mother talking."

"Of course they would be worried about what might happen to you," Clara said.

"Not to me or us," Gunther said. "To you."

"What?"

"To you and your family. My mother and father are very much afraid you could be hurt, or worse."

Clara didn't say anything. She had spent all night worried about the exact same thing.

"I am worried too," Gunther said, and averted his face as if embarrassed.

"That's sweet," Clara said.

They fell silent.

Clara was pleased that Gunther was talking to her and wanted to keep him talking so she said the first thing that popped into her head. "Plus there's Indians."

"*Ja.* Yes. My father says some tribes are not friendly. We could be on their land and not know it."

"My pa says Indians don't own land like we do. He says they roam all over."

"Still, they might not like us being here."

"You speak English real good," Clara complimented him.

"I speak German too," Gunther said. "Mostly I learned it from my grandmother when I was little. She is dead now."

"What do you want to be when you grow up?"

Gunther looked at her and grinned. "You ask many questions. Is it because you are a girl?"

Clara laughed. "Everybody asks questions."

"I do not know what I will do," Gunther said. "Except I do not care to live in these mountains. I like back in the States."

"Me too."

They both smiled, and Clara felt closer to him than she ever did. All her friends back to home were girls but she reckoned it might be nice to have a boy as a friend, too. "I guess if we live close to each other we'll grow up together."

"And when we are old enough, we could leave together."

Clara nearly tripped over own feet. "What?"

"If you still want to go to the East to live. I would help you get there."

"Thank you." Clara was feeling strangely warm all over. Afraid she might be blushing, she gazed all about them so he couldn't see her face. To the west. To the south. Over her shoulder.

Clara stopped stone still.

Gunther took a couple more steps and then he stopped, too. "What is the matter?"

"I thought....," Clara said, too stunned to finish.

Her family's covered wagon clattered on, the chickens in the cage clucking noisily. The Walberg wagon approached, the oxen paying her and Gunther no mind.

Mrs. Walberg was walking along the side and she smiled and said, "What are you children doing just standing there?"

"We were talking, mother," Gunther said.

"Well, keep up," Mrs. Walberg said. She patted

Clara on the arm as she went by. "We don't want to lose you." She laughed merrily.

Clara stayed rooted in place.

"What is it?" Gunther whispered.

"I thought....," Clara said again. She tried telling herself she must be mistaken. It was her imagination, her ma would say.

"Are you sick or something?"

Clara blurted it out. "I think I saw the bear."

"The grizzly from last night?"

Clara nodded. "On that rise down yonder."

Gunther looked. "There's nothing. Grass and a few trees."

"It was there and it was gone," Clara said. Just like last night. She couldn't understand how something so huge could vanish so quickly.

"Are you sure?"

Clara was honest with him. "Well, no. Not to where I'd swear on the Bible."

"It could have been something else," Gunther said. "A black bear. They are common in these mountains, too. Or an elk. My father tells me they are plentiful."

"I suppose." Tired of talking about it, Clara wheeled and headed after the wagons.

Gunther wasn't done. "Besides. Why would the grizzly follow us? There is game everywhere."

"True," Clara conceded.

The wagons were winding up a slight grade toward a ridge. As laden as they were, the oxen had to strain mightily the last fifty yards. Once over the crest, her pa called a halt. He and Mr. Walberg roved back and forth, studying the way ahead.

STALKED

Clara hunkered and folded her arms. To her, the slopes above were much too steep for their wagons or any others. She hoped her pa would see the error of his ways and agree to turn around and rejoin the wagon train.

Her ma and Mrs. Walberg were standing in the shade of the Walberg's wagon. Alice and Hermann were by the water barrel. Jacob was tending to the oxen.

Since no one needed her for anything, Clara squatted and plucked at some grass.

Gunther did the same.

"You're sticking awful close to me today," Clara remarked.

Gunther shrugged. "Who else would I talk to? Hermann thinks I am just a kid."

"We are," Clara said, grinning. On an impulse, she stood and turned and walked to the slope they had climbed.

The view was magnificent. To the north and south ran the foothills. Beyond spread the prairie. Hawks wheeled in the sky below. An eagle soared with outstretched wings. A few deer were in a clearing, grazing.

"I do so love the animals," Clara said.

"Just not grizzlies," Gunther said.

They laughed, and Clara was beginning to relax when movement in woods that flanked the last hill they had climbed drew her attention. Something big was in the shadows. She couldn't quite make it out. She pointed. "Do you see that?"

The movement stopped.

"I only see trees," Gunther said.

Clara began to wonder about herself. This made twice now she could have sworn she saw something. Before she could say more to Gunther, there was a commotion at the wagons and her ma yelled for her to come quick.

Mrs. Walberg did the same for Gunther.

He turned but Clara hesitated, hoping the thing in the woods would show itself.

"Clara Gordon! Get over here this instant!"

Her mother's tone startled her.

Clara swiveled around and was puzzled to see nearly everyone standing rigid and staring fixedly up the mountain. She glanced up and a tingle shot through her.

Indians were approaching. Three of them, on horseback, the youngest leading another horse laden with furs.

All the stories Clara heard tell about the terrible things Indians did to whites welled up. Fear lent her speed as she ran to her mother, who had an arm around Alice's shoulders and now put the other arm around Clara.

"Stay still and don't speak," her ma said. "Let the men handle this."

Mrs. Walberg and Gunther were watching in fascination and unease.

Hermann and Jacob were by the oxen, both with their rifles.

Clara's pa and Mr. Walberg had taken their rifles and moved in front of the wagons. They held their rifles ready to use but didn't point them at the Indians.

"What tribe are they?" Mr. Walberg said.

"How would I know?" her pa replied. "I just pray they're friendly."

So did Clara. She'd heard that sometimes Indians went around in war parties killing everybody they came across. She didn't know how many were in a 'party' but she hoped it was more than three. "We should smile and act nice."

"I told you to hush," her ma said, and gave her a shake.

The Indians spread out and came on riding abreast.

"If they attack, get the kids under the wagons," her pa said to her ma.

"What good would that do?" Alice said.

"Can't either of you do as you're told?" her ma said, and gave Alice a shake, too.

"I wish we knew the tribe," Mr. Walberg said.

Clara resisted an urge to press against her mother. She refused to show she was afraid. She stood straight and jutted her chin out.

The Indians came on calmly. Two had bows and quivers of arrows and the third held a lance with feathers attached. As they came up and drew rein, the third one pointed his lance at her father.

Chapter 4

Nate King was in fine spirits.

For the first time in a long while, he and the love of his life---and their adopted daughter---were making their leisurely way down from the high country toward the distant plains. Their destination was a favorite place of his. Bent's Fort. He would stock up on supplies and mingle with the traders and freighters and others to hear the latest news from back East and whatever other news of the frontier was being bandied about.

Nate sat his bay with an ease born of long experience. His Hawken was cradled in the crook of his arm. Pistols were wedged under his wide leather belt on either side of the buckle, as was a tomahawk on his right hip. A Bowie hung from a beaded sheath on his left. His buckskins were beaded, too, courtesy of Winona and her superb skill at fashioning their clothes.

Nate shifted in his saddle to regard the one he adored with affection.

Winona noticed, and smiled. "I know that look, husband." Her own beaded dress was a fine example of her craftsmanship. She, too, cradled a Hawken, custom-made for her by the Hawken brothers years ago. Her features were typical of her people, the

Shoshones, but to Nate she was one of the most beautiful women alive. Her long black hair was greying at the temples although her face showed no wrinkles as of yet.

"You should," Nate teased, "As long as we've been together."

"Many winters," Winona said. "And we have two fine children who are now fully grown."

Nate would prefer not to be reminded of how fast the time went by.

Over a year ago, his youngest, Evelyn, became hitched to a young man she had mooned over since she met him.

Their oldest, Zach, had a youngun of his own.

That would have left Nate and Winona with an empty nest except that Winona had taken a shine to a Tukudeka girl who lost her parents and decided to adopt the girl as their own.

Bright Rainbow was her name. She had seen fourteen winters but she was mature for her age. She posed no problems for them whatsoever.

Now she saw Nate staring at her and she smiled and raised her hand.

Nate smiled. Life was good. As, ideally, it should be when a man and woman were fifty or more. At that age people should be able to take life a little easier and enjoy the fruits of their younger years.

That wasn't always the case, especially in the wilds. The wilderness was a harsh mistress. She demanded constant vigilance. Letting down one's guard was an invite to calamity. A lesson Nate had learned many times over. Which was why he rode with his senses fully alert and never stopped gazing every which way to ensure they weren't taken by surprise.

So it was that he caught sight of three riders and a pack animal far down below before the riders caught sight of them.

Instantly, he signaled for Winona and Bright Rainbow to follow his lead and reined over near a stand of aspens.

"What?" Winona said.

"Men below," Bright Rainbow said. "On horses." She had been learning to speak English and was better at it every day.

Once again Nate was impressed by how dependable the girl was. The girl was always aware of everything and anything going on around her. Maybe it had something to do with losing her mother and father in so grisly a manner.

"Which tribe?" Winona wondered.

"Let's find out," Nate said. Opening his parfleche, he rummaged inside and took out a collapsible brass spyglass. Back in his early days as a fur trapper it would have come in mighty handy. He could have avoided more than a few war parties and other perils.

Extending the telescope, he fixed it on the trio yonder. The distance was such that he still couldn't tell much. If he had to guess, he would say they were Utes. Then again, they might be Blackfeet from off to the north or from another unfriendly tribe.

Indian territories weren't set in stone. Warriors roamed wide afield in search of enemies or to hunt or simply to satisfy their curiosity about what lay over the next hill or mountain.

"Well?" Winona said.

"Can't tell," Nate said.

"We can avoid them by swinging south," Winona said. "They will never know we were here."

Nate nodded. It was smart to go out of their way to avoid a clash. Although he had acquired the name Grizzly Killer on his initial foray into the mountains and was known as a formidable fighter, he would prefer to not spill blood if he could help it.

Bright Rainbow came up next to them. "What is that?" she asked, pointing.

Nate had been so intent on the three warriors that he hadn't noticed tendrils of dust rising from further down. He raised his spyglass again and frowned as the source of the dust became apparent. "Wonderful. Just wonderful," he muttered.

"What are you grumbling about, husband?" Winona said.

"Settlers," Nate said, not bothering to hide his annoyance. Of late, it seemed as if every time he turned around, more showed up.

"With wagons?"

Nate nodded.

"How did they get so far in?" Winona said.

Nate shrugged. Anyone with a lick of common sense would know better than to try and penetrate deep into the mountains with a covered wagon. It couldn't be done. Not in this section of the Rockies. The only way was to cross over at South Pass, which was many miles to the north, on a trail that ultimately wound up in Oregon Country.

Nate focused on the covered wagons. He made out

figures walking beside them. Men. Women. And smaller ones. "They have children."

"How many?"

"Hard to say at this distance."

"The warriors have seen them," Bright Rainbow said.

"That they have," Nate agreed. To Winona he said, "You know what that means?" He didn't wait for an answer. "We can't swing south. We have to do what we can for those pilgrims. The warriors might be hostile."

"Let us hope they are friendly," Winona said.

Nate flicked his reins. As best he could tell, the settlers were half a mile or so lower than the Indians. It could well be the settlers had no idea the warriors were there. In which case they would plod right into an ambush.

Nate rode faster than he would have liked. He avoided a talus slope and entered a tract of tall pines where a carpet of needles muffled the thud of their mounts' hooves.

Winona stayed close behind him, her long hair flying.

Bright Rainbow was inscrutable, as always. She rode well even though she hadn't sat a horse much when she was little.

Hard riding brought them to a ridge. Nate drew rein and slid down. He calculated they were close enough to the warriors that he should be able to tell more about them. His spyglass in hand, he moved to the rim.

Winona and Bright Rainbow quickly joined him.

"The warriors have stopped," the girl said.

STALKED

That they had. They were watching the covered wagons.

A quarter-mile lower, the settlers slogged at a snail's pace. Their oxen were struggling, and the steepest slopes were yet to come.

Nate's initial guess was right. The warriors were Utes. Whether they were friendly or not depended on which band they were from. Some weren't fond of all the white intruders.

Nate had tangled with the Utes a few times during his early days in the Rockies. They were a proud people. Decades back, they were known as keen traders. Then the Spanish came along and the Utes acquired horses, and their lives were never the same. They became adept at breeding and riding---and as feared warriors. It go so, a man's standing in the tribe was tied to how many horses he owned. Own a lot, and that warrior, to put it in white man terms, was rich and powerful.

They defended their land fiercely. Not as savagely as, say, the Apaches. Nor were they as prone to go on the war path, as, say, the Blackfeet. But no one took them lightly, as nearly everyone did, say, the Otoes. The latter were farmers with no interest in war and as a consequence were being exterminated by their warlike neighbors.

"There, husband," Winona said, indicating a strip of forest that would screen them until they caught up to the Utes.

Nate nodded. He was the first to his horse and led the way down a gradual slope at the south end of the ridge. Once in the forest, he threaded through the trees until they drew abreast of where the three warriors waited.

The Utes were talking among themselves, with a lot of gesturing. They didn't appear to be about to attack.

Nate reckoned they were debating whether to show themselves to the whites. It wouldn't surprise him if they decided not to. They couldn't be sure of their reception. It wasn't uncommon for whites to shoot at Indians on sight.

As for the settlers, they were still oblivious. In Sioux country they wouldn't last a week. They were literally babes in the woods. That such infants had the gall to think they could make a go of it in the Rockies never ceased to amaze him.

Then again, Nate had been just like them, once.

"What do we do?" Winona whispered.

"Wait." Nate wasn't eager for them to show themselves just yet. He'd rather wait and see what developed. It could be there wasn't any cause for concern. The Utes might prove friendly and the whites might welcome them peaceably.

In which case Nate and his family could be on their way.

"Look," Bright Rainbow said.

The oldest of the warriors had gigged his mount and was descending toward the covered wagons. His friends flanked him to either side.

Incredibly, the settlers still hadn't noticed them.

Winona looked at Nate and shook her head in disbelief.

"I know," Nate said. He paralleled the Utes, staying as near to them as he could without giving himself and his wife and daughter away.

"There!" Bright Rainbow said.

One of the women finally glanced up and saw the Indians. She yelled, and suddenly all the whites were darting about.

Two men with rifles moved to the forefront. One wore a black hat and had curly black hair, the other was portly.

Two boys placed themselves near the first team of oxen.

The women held back with the children, all clearly terrified.

"Let's hope the men aren't quick on the trigger," Winona said.

Thankfully, the whites were holding their fire. But they looked as nervous as could be.

The Utes slowed and presently drew rein.

"They show no hostility whatsoever," Winona said.

No sooner were the words out of her mouth than the Ute leader raised his lance toward one of the settlers.

And the settler in the black hat jerked his rifle up.

Chapter 5

Nate broke from cover at a gallop. "Don't shoot!" he hollered. "They're not hostiles!"

The whites and the Utes reacted alike. They froze in surprise, the oldest warrior with his lance extended, the settler with his rifle pointed. The women and children were likewise transfixed.

Nate galloped up and drew sharp rein closer to the warriors than to the wagons. Behind him came Winona and Bright Rainbow, adding to the general amazement.

"Don't shoot!" Nate said again to the settler with his rifle pointed. "There's no need for bloodshed." To the Utes he said in their tongue, "We are friends."

The settlers and the warriors exchanged looks, and the man pointing the rifle slowly lowered it. "You sure it's safe, mister?"

"They won't harm you," Nate assured him. He turned to the Ute leader and quickly signed, "Lower your lance. The whites think you mean to attack them."

"I wanted only to talk," the oldest Ute said.

"I know," Nate said.

"You speak our tongue?" the Ute said.

"A little," Nate said. Mostly he relied on sign language. Winona was the linguist in the family. So much so, her grasp of English was better than this own.

"I am called Sapariche. How are you known?"

"Your people and others know me as Grizzly Killer," Nate signed. A name he was given decades ago by a Cheyenne warrior who saw him slay a griz, more by luck than anything.

The warriors began talking among themselves as Nate turned back to the whites. "Nate King," he said. "We were passing by."

"King, you say?" the man in the black hat said. "I heard that name mentioned by a scout not long ago." He smiled. "I'm Charles Gordon. I've brought my family to the Rockies to live."

"So I see," Nate said. It was as plain as the nose on his face that they were as green as grass. He was tempted to tell them they should turn around and head back while they still could but he held his tongue.

"Nate King," Charles Gordon said again. "The scout told us you live deep in the mountains. Deeper than anyone."

"I like my privacy," Nate said. "Hold on a second." He turned back to the Utes, who were regarding him with keen interest. Again he resorted to sign. "I can speak to the whites for you if you want."

Sapariche studied Nate closely. "You say you are the white known as Grizzly Killer?" he signed.

"Yes."

"The same Grizzly Killer who helped Neota and his people by slaying the grizzly known as Scar?"

"Yes."

"I am honored to meet you," Sapariche signed. "You truly are a friend of the Utes." He turned toward the whites. "Why are they here?"

"They came to the mountains to live," Nate explained.

"Have the whites used up all the land where they come from?"

"No," Nate said.

"Is it not far, their land?"

"Yes."

Sapariche twisted on his mount and and gazed up at the steep slopes and high peaks. "Yet they come here?"

Nate almost laughed at how incredulous he sounded. "Yes."

"Are they like you, these whites? Do they have great courage and are strong fighters?"

"I do not know them," Nate signed.

Sapariche signed, "They do not look strong. They were afraid of us. I could see it on their faces. They should not have come. The mountains will kill them, I think."

"You might speak truth," Nate signed.

Sapariche smiled. "Do not take offense, Grizzly Killer. I have observed that whites often walk around with their heads in a whirl."

Nate grinned. "I am an adopted Shoshone."

Sapariche and the other two Utes smiled.

"What's so funny?" Charles Gordon asked. "What have you been talking about with your fingers and all?"

"The Utes were wondering why you are here," Nate said.

"Utes, are they? Never heard of them," Charles said. "And I came for the same reason you did."

"Is that so?"

Charles nodded. "I hankered after a new life for me and mine. A place where I was beholden to no one but myself. Where we could live as we pleased. Do as we pleased. That's why you came, I bet."

"I came because an uncle told me he could make me rich," Nate said.

"But you stayed," Charles said. "You must have had a good reason."

Nate looked at Winona. "I do."

Charles gestured at the warriors. "Should I give them something? As a peace offering? We don't have much to spare but maybe some eggs or flour or, I don't know, a shirt?"

"I have whiskey," the other man said. "I'm Otto Walberg, by the way."

"No whiskey," Nate said gruffly. He was thinking of an incident some years back where a man set up a trading post and a lot of warriors started sucking it down as if it were water. "You don't have to give them anything. They're not after handouts."

"I want to," Charles said. "To show I'm friendly. Let them know they can stop by my place any time they want once I've settled in."

Nate, impressed, relayed the information. Many settlers, out of sheer fear, would want nothing to do with Indians.

Sapariche was apparently impressed, too. "He speaks with a straight tongue, this one?"

"I believe so," Nate signed.

"Tell him I will take his offer of friendship to heart," Sapariche signed. "There will be peace between his lodge and mine."

Nate did as the Ute requested.

"How about that?" Charles Gordon said to Walberg. "We haven't even built our cabins yet and we've made peace with the Indians."

"Only with Sapariche," Nate set him straight.

"But he'll tell his friends and his tribe will be less likely to want to harm us, yes?" Charles anxiously asked.

"You made a wise choice," Nate said.

Charles beamed, proud of himself, and glanced at his wife.

She didn't seem nearly as delighted.

Sapariche had long believed that whites behaved in a ridiculous manner. They did such strange things. Acted in such strange ways.

These whites with their wagons were more proof. Taking their families into the mountains where hardly any other whites were to be found. They would be alone, cut off from their own kind. Should the Blackfeet or the Bloods come across them, they would be easy prey.

Perhaps he was judging too harshly, Sapariche told himself. Perhaps they were good hunters and the women knew all about skinning and turning hides into clothes. Perhaps. But he very much doubted it.

As the white in the black hat showed all his teeth to everyone, Sapariche signed to Grizzly Killer that they were leaving.

"So soon?" Grizzly Killer signed. "You are welcome at our fire."

Sapariche was pleased. White men who understood

the ways of his people and other tribes like the Shoshones were rare. "Another day," he signed.

"You go to hunt buffalo?"

"To Bent's Fort," Sapariche said. He was eager to continue on. He and his brother and nephew had been away from their village for ten sleeps. He looked forward to completing their journey so they could trade for items they wanted and then return to their loved ones.

"We go there as well," Grizzly Killer revealed.

Sapariche was doubly pleased. He had heard so much about this man. Here was an opportunity to get to know him. "We can travel together."

Grizzly Killer raised his hands to sign, then hesitated. He stared at the white men and their families, then turned to his Shoshone wife, who said something in the white tongue. Grizzly Killer nodded, and signed, "I would very much like to. But we will stay and talk to these people. Perhaps we will see you at the fort."

"I hope so," Sapariche signed. He smiled at the silly whites and reined around them and headed on down the foothills.

His brother and nephew, Tishawat and Ungamo, trailed after him, Ungamo tugging on the lead rope to their pack horse.

None of them spoke until they reached the top of a hill lower down and drew rein to look back.

"I will never understand whites," Tishawat said. "They are like birds that flit about in the bushes."

Sapariche grinned.

"We met Grizzly Killer!" Ungamo declared. "The stories they tell of him. How he risked his life to help our people."

"Were it not for him, many more of Neota's band would have died," Sapariche said. He watched the great wagons that made him think of a turtle move slowly up the mountain, Grizzly Killer and his family riding beside them. "I hope we see him at Bent's Fort. I would like to hear from his own lips how he killed Scar."

They resumed their trek.

Sapariche enjoyed the serenity of the countryside. The vivid blue of the clear sky. The green of the rolling foothills, broken here and there by the red of sandstone cliffs. The distant prairie with its unending grass. Dots on the horizon that might be buffalo. A white-headed eagle soared on high. A pair of ravens glided and cawed.

Moments like this, Sapariche reflected, were to be savored. Life was unpredictable. A man never knew but when an enemy might appear, or a threat in the natural order of things would loom.

They wound lower.

Abruptly, his brother stopped and tilted his head and sniffed. "Do you smell that?"

Sapariche sniffed, to no avail. His brother always did have a better nose. "What is it you smell?"

"Bear," Tishawat said. He indicated thick forest not an arrow's flight off. "In there."

"Which kind? Black or silver-tip?"

"I am not a wolf that I can tell the difference," Tishawat said.

"I will go see," Ungamo said.

"Stay with us, son," Tishawat said. "The bear is leaving us alone. We should leave it alone."

Sapariche agreed. "Why look for trouble when

trouble is not looking for you?" He rode on but kept his eyes on the forest. Bears were not to be taken lightly. Not the humped ones, anyway. They were the most fearsome creatures in all the mountains. Arrows and lances could not always stop them.

"When we stop for the night we should find somewhere easy to defend," Tishawat said.

"Do you think the bear will attack us, father?" Ungamo said.

"No. To be safe, though."

Sapariche made light of it by saying, "In all my winters I have never been attacked by a bear. I would not like to start now."

His brother and his nephew laughed.

Chapter 6

The covered wagons were parked in a half-circle at the open end of the clearing. Nate suggested it as an extra precaution.

At the moment a fire was crackling and a stew pot hung from a tripod. Elizabeth Gordon was stirring the stew.

Charles Gordon and his son Jacob and daughters Alice and Clara sat to one side of the fire. Otto Walbert and his wife Freida, along with their sons Hermann and Gunthers, were on the other side.

One and all were staring at Nate, Winona and Bright Rainbow as if they were alien creatures who had just appeared out of the ether.

Nate found it amusing.

"I want to thank you again for coming with us a ways," Charles Gordon said for about the sixth time since Nate had stopped him from shooting Sapariche.

"We thought it might be best," Nate said. Actually, it was Winona who up and told him they should tag along for a spell. Which figured. She had a heart a mile wide.

"We welcome any advice you can give us, Mr. King," Otto Walberg said in his clipped accent.

'Short of turning around and going back?' Nate almost said. Instead, he responded with, "How far in do you plan to go?"

"As far as you," Charles said.

Nate shook his head. "Not possible."

"Why not?" Elizabeth Gordon said.

"You'd never make it," Nate informed them. "Not with those heavy wagons. We packed everything in on horses."

"Do you have a suggestion as to where we might build our cabins?" Otto Walberg said. "You must know these mountains very well."

Winona answered before Nate could. "I have been thinking about that since we met you. Wherever you settle, there should be water and grass as well as plenty of timber."

"Know of a spot?" Charles said.

Winona said. "My husband and I know of one, yes. In a small valley that would be perfect for you. It is two days in from here and has a stream that runs year round."

"Some don't?" Freida Walberg said.

"Many do not," Winona said. "The summers are long and hot and there is not much rain. By fall they can be trickles or less."

"You'd guide us to this valley?" Charles excitedly asked.

Nate looked at Winona, who nodded.

Elizabeth Gordon noticed. "We appreciate you being so helpful, Mrs. King. Us being strangers and all."

"Call me Winona, please."

"That's a pretty name. You're Shoshone, your husband told us?"

"Yes," Winona said. "But my name is not."

"How did that come about?" Elizabeth said.

"About the time I was to be born, a popular name for girls among my people, the Shoshone, was Wini," Winona related. "My mother was going to name me that. Then our band met with another who had a little Sioux girl with them. Their warriors had come across her wandering lost on the prairie and brought her back. Her name was Winona. My mother liked the name so much, she persuaded my father to let her name me that."

"Do you like your name, Mrs. King?" Alice said. "I never much liked mine. It's so ordinary."

"Honestly, Alice," Elizabeth said.

"This valley," Charles said. "Is it near an Indian village?"

"No," Nate set him at ease. "It's in Ute territory but as you've already seen, they can be friendly when you're friendly to them." He paused. "Plus it's only about a two-week ride from Bent's Fort."

"Only?" Freida Walberg said.

"Out here that's the same as being next door," Nate said.

"Sounds almost too good to be true," Charles said happily. "I can't believe our luck in running into you."

"The Good Lord is watching over us," Elizabeth said. She stirred the stew, then raised the spoon and tested the soup. "Supper will be ready in a bit."

"Thank you for shooting that rabbit, Mr. King," Otto Walberg said. "Fresh meat is welcome."

"You have to stay alert for food for your pot," Nate advised. "And you'll need to learn how to jerk meat for winter if you don't already know."

"There is much we must learn," Freida Walberg said.

"And we will," Otto declared. "We will do whatever is needed to live as comfortably as we can."

"You're staying, then?" Charles asked.

"Mr. King has made up my mind for me," Otto said. "If he can do it, we can do it. So, yes, we stay and will be your neighbors."

Nate was tempted to point out that there was a considerable difference between their situation and his. He'd learned to survive first from his uncle and then from seasoned frontiersmen Shakespeare McNair.

"Wait!" Elizabeth exclaimed, and turned to the east, and the rolling foothills below. "Did you hear that? It sounded like a scream!"

Sapariche wanted to stop early. His horse was tired and so he was he. He wasn't a young man anymore. He had seen over sixty winters. Had shared his lodge with two wives and raised four children.

His first wife died when a horse kicked her in the head. It was one of those things no one could predict or prevent. She was seated near the horses, mending a cradleboard, when a horsefly bit a mare on the flank. The mare reacted by kicking out with its rear legs and a hoof caught his wife in the back of he skull and caved it in.

Life did that. Life gave you happy days and sad days. That was the saddest in all his experience. He was younger then, and another woman was interested in him even though he had two children. So he took her into his lodge and she bore him two more. All told, he had two daughters and two sons.

He had hoped his sons would accompany him to Bent's Fort but neither was able. Fortunately, his brother and nephew were interested. He would not have dared it alone.

Yet another mark of age. When he was younger and a warrior in the full vigor of his youth and strength, he had done much that he now regarded as folly. He had taken foolish chances. Done foolish things. That he survived was due more to luck than anything.

Now, winding lower among the foothills as the sun dipped toward the western rampart of mountains, Sapariche smiled at his memories.

"There," Tishawat suddenly said, extending an arm. "Our camp for the night."

The slope they were descending ended on a flat bench. A short wall of rock, where erosion had worn away much of the earth, made an ideal shelter from the wind. Even better, and rarer, was a small spring. It was perfect for them and their horses.

"I will hunt for our meal," Ungamo offered, hefting his bow. Swinging down, he gave the reins to his horse to his father.

"Be on the watch for the bear," Sapariche said.

"I have not smelled it in a long while," Tishawat said. "We left it up the mountain."

Sliding an arrow from his quiver, Ungamo notched it to his bow's sinew string, smiled at them, and glided toward the forest.

"Perhaps you should go with him," Sapariche said.

"He is a grown man," Tishawat said. "He would be

insulted."

They watered their animals and tied them, then entered the forest to gather wood for their fire. The sun was half gone and murky shadows lent the woods a sinister aspect.

Sapariche shook off the feeling and proceeded to fill his arms with downed limbs he broke to a suitable size. There were plenty, enough to last the whole night.

They were heading back when Tishawat gave a slight start and twisted to stare into the gathering gloom.

"Something?" Sapariche said.

"I thought I smelled the bear again." Tishawat sniffed loudly.

"Do you still smell it?"

"No. It was there and it was gone." Tishawat scowled. "I will be glad when my son returns."

"If there was trouble he would have yelled," Sapariche said.

Tishawat grunted.

Sapariche kindled the fire while his brother stood waiting for Ungamo. Barely a thin ribbon of sun remained when the undergrowth crackled and Ungamo emerged carrying two squirrels by their tails.

Smiling, Ungamo held them up. "We will eat well."

"How went the hunt?" Tishawat said.

"They were easy," Ungamo said as he sank to his knees, set down his bow, and drew his knife. "I put an arrow in one when it was on the ground near a tree and the other when it came around the tree to see what happened."

"Did you hear or see anything else?" Tishawat said.

"A doe but she ran off." Ungamo bent to begin skinning.

Sapariche was seated with his back to the rock wall, facing the fire. A full belly would help him sleep. They would be on their way early and well out on the prairie by midday.

His nephew made short work of the skinning and soon both squirrels were on spits over the fire.

The aroma of roasting flesh made Sapariche's mouth water. Squirrel was a favorite. The taste was a little like rabbit only sweeter. He often thought it a shame that squirrels weren't as big as buffalo. He would eat them and nothing else.

Twilight gave way to full night.

Once the squirrels were nicely brown, Ungamo passed the meat around.

Sapariche chewed with relish. Some of the juice dripped from the corner of his mouth and he licked it with his tongue.

When they were almost done, Tishawat remarked, "Wait until our families and friends hear we met Grizzly Killer."

That got them talking about whites they knew of who had been adopted by different tribes. Then about whites in general. And finally about the whites with the huge wagons.

"If they are alive two winters from now I will be surprised," Tishawat said.

Sapariche's eyelids were growing heavy. He announced that he was turning in and lay on his side with his back to the fire. He listened to his brother and nephew until the drone of their voices put him to sleep

He couldn't say what woke him.

His eyes were open and the rock wall was in front of him. Judging by the diminished glow, the fire had burned low. He was about to sit up and add firewood when he heard a sound that caused his heart to leap in his chest.

It was a loud crunch. As of teeth on bone.

Sapariche's mouth went dry. He was going to say his brother's name but stopped himself. There was another crunch, even louder.

Careful not to move his body and give himself away, Sapariche ever so slowly turned his head. He nearly gasped when he saw his brother's head.

Just the head.

It lay an arm's length away, the neck a jagged ruin. Then he saw his brother's body and the thing that was crunching bone.

It was the father of all bears. The largest grizzly Sapariche ever set eyes on. He stayed still, afraid that if he moved, the bear would be on him before he could gain his feet.

He couldn't understand how the bear slew his brother without waking him. Had he been sleeping that soundly?

Sapariche wondered what happened to his nephew. No sooner did he think that than there was a loud groan.

He shifted his eyes and smothered an outcry.

Ungamo lay on his side beyond the flickering fire, his back to the flames. The rear of his head was bloody and the back of his shirt had been ripped wide.

Sapariche guessed that his nephew had been

keeping watch and fallen asleep sitting up and the bear had come up behind him and felled him and then moved on to Tishawat.

Sapariche heard another groan and his nephew jerked and rolled over, blinking and grimacing.

The great bear raised its enormous head. A couple of ponderous steps and it stood over Ungamo.

His nephew tried to rise but was slammed flat by a huge paw. Slammed so hard that at least one of his ribs gave an audible crack.

Ungamo did the only thing he could.

He screamed.

Chapter 7

Nate King straightened and listened intently. It sounded like a scream to him, too. It was faint, though, so faint it faded out and in again several times. The wind was to blame, he suspected.

The Gordon and Walberg families were on their feet, peering into the night. Some in stark fear.

"Is that a person?" Freida Walberg said.

"Hard to tell," Jacob Gordon said.

"Sounded like one to me," Elizabeth said, protectively draping her arm across her youngest daughter's shoulders.

Her oldest daughter, Alice, shuddered. "Whatever it is, I don't like it."

Charles sought to soothe her with, "Whatever or whoever made that is way off. It's nothing for us to fret about."

"I never heard a sound like that in all my life," Otto Walberg said.

"Me either, father," Hermann said.

Nate exchanged looks with Winona. He imagined that she was thinking the same thing he was, namely, that the scream came from the direction the three Ute warriors had gone. Could it have been one of them? He very much doubted it. Ute warriors were tough. He never heard tell of one screaming, not even in the heat and blood of violent combat.

"What do you think, Mr. King?" Elizabeth said. "Is it something we should be worried about?"

"I shouldn't think so," Nate said. Even if the Utes had run into enemies, there was no reason to expect their adversaries would backtrack them and come after the settlers.

"I agree," Winona said. "To ease your worries, my husband and I, and our daughter, will stay with you for several days. We have considerable experience in dealing with any and all problems that might arise."

"You would do that for us?" Freida Walberg said.

"We would do it for anyone," Winona replied.

"By problems you mean hostiles?" Charles said.

"Those too," Winona said.

To Nate's surprise, young Clara came around the fire and stood in front of him.

"Clara, what are you doing?" Elizabeth Gordon said.

The girl bent toward Nate and said almost in a whisper, "Do you deal with bears?"

"Excuse me?" Nate said.

"Bears," Clara said. "Big bears."

Charles Gordon chuckled. "We saw a grizzly last night. She's been scared to death ever since."

"What did it do?" Nate said.

"Do?" Charles said. "Nothing. It came up on us when we were camped. Looked at us and went off. Didn't so much as growl. That was it."

"Perhaps it was only curious," Winona said.

"You were lucky," Nate said. They didn't know *how* lucky. Grizzlies were the most formidable creatures in the Rockies. As Lewis and Clark had discovered, they were incredibly difficult to kill. 'Hard to die', Lewis said of them, and if ever there was an understatement, that was it.

Nate knew of a grizzly that took fourteen or more lead balls and didn't go down.

To make matters worse, they were as unpredictable as they were fierce. Where one might catch sight of a human and run off, the next might chase the human down and treat itself to a meal.

"We have our rifles and our pistols," Charles said confidently. "And I'm a fair shot, if I do say so myself. So is my son, Jacob."

Jacob grinned and nodded.

"Hermann and I will shoot if we have to," Otto Walberg said.

"You must know all about grizzlies," Charles said. "How many have you killed, anyhow?"

"Not that many," Nate said. He wasn't about to relate every encounter he'd ever had.

"Any advice you can give us, Mr. King?" Elizabeth said.

"If they're not out to eat you, let them go their way and you go yours," Nate said. "If they come after you, try to get up a good-sized tree they can't push over. As heavy as they are, they can't climb. The adults, anyway." He realized Clara was still staring up at him. "Anything else, little one?"

"I wish we were back in South Carolina," the girl said.

"Clara Gordon!" Elizabeth said.

"I do, ma," Clara said.

"Quit your moping, girl," Charles said. "We're here to stay and that's final." To Nate he said, "She's been pining for home since we left. Can't blame her, I guess. Pulling up roots can be hard on a person."

Nate's estimation of the man rose a notch.

"It was hard on us, too," Freida Walberg said. "But all the talk about Oregon Country swayed us. They say it is a new Promised Land."

"Yet you didn't go all the way," Nate noted.

"My husband believes we can make a go of it here and I have faith in him."

"Don't you worry, Mrs. Walberg," Charles said. "Everything will work out just fine. You'll see."

For all their sakes, Nate hoped so.

Sapariche could not get his arms or legs to move. He wanted to jump up and go to his nephew's aid but his body betrayed him.

The grizzly snorted and shook its head as if in annoyance.

Only when Sapariche saw its massive jaws open and snap shut on his nephew's throat, cutting off Ungamo's scream, was he able to will his body into motion. Flattening on his belly, he crawled toward the welcome darkness beyond the firelight. His only hope to live was in sneaking away while the bear was occupied.

A loud gurgle from Ungamo drew his gaze. His poor nephew was convulsing.

The bear raised its head and sniffed.

Sapariche turned to stone. If the grizzly turned in his direction he was doomed. But no. It gnawed at the soft flesh of Ungamo's throat, then slurped noisily.

Sapariche resumed crawling. If he could make it to the forest he would scramble as fast as he was able up a suitable tree. To hide in the thick brush would be pointless. The bear would smell him out no matter how thick the vegetation might be.

Fortunately, the fire was so low that he wouldn't need to crawl far to be out of the light.

Sapariche fought an urge to crawl faster. He must not make any noise. The bear would hear and be on him before he could hope to flee.

He stared at the forest and nothing else.

When a leg with a hoof attached blocked his view, it startled him.

He looked up, and could have kicked himself. He was so upset by the death of his brother and his nephew that he wasn't thinking clearly.

He had completely forgotten about their horses.

The four animals were still tied to their stakes. Riveted by the bear, they were only now stirring to life.

One nervously raised a leg and brought its hoof down not a finger's length from Sapariche. Another whinnied.

The grizzly went on chewing at Ungamo.

Sapariche came to a quick decision. A horse was better than a tree. His own animal was at the end of the string but his nephew's, the horse that almost trod on him, was right there, within easy reach.

Pushing up into a crouch, Sapariche groped at the stake, gripped it with both hands, and pulled. Ordinarily stakes would slide right out but his nephew had the habit of driving them too deeply into the ground out of worry his horse might stray off in the night.

Sapariche grit his teeth and pulled harder.

All four horses neighed or nickered and tugged at their ropes.

With good cause.

The grizzly was looking over at them, a strip of skin dangling from its mouth.

Sapariche's blood became ice. He strained with all his might and the stake popped out, nearly throwing him off balance. He snatched the leather tether and started to rise so he could climb on. But he wasn't quite fast enough.

The bear was coming toward the horses.

Panicked horses were difficult to control. And these were terrified. Frantic, they sought to pull free from the stakes.

Two of the horses---Sapariche's and his brother's---were war horses, trained to perform in warfare without fear. But even they were terrified. The grizzly was almost as big and heavy as they were, and with its teeth and claws, a behemoth of destruction. Against that, a horse had its flailing hooves and its own teeth, neither as effective.

The grizzly growled, a low, ominous rumble that prickled the short hairs at the nape of Sapariche's neck.

He glanced over his shoulder.

The bear was looking at him, not at the horses.

Sapariche grabbed at the mane of the animal he had freed, intending to grab hold and vault up, only to have the horse suddenly sidestep and slam into him, driven against him by the frenzied movements of the other horses.

STALKED

He tripped and staggered but recovered and flung both arms over the animal's back.

The horse reared.

Unable to brace himself, Sapariche was sent sprawling. He landed between that horse and the next and jerked aside as a hoof thumped into the earth. He rolled, seeking to get out of there, and collided with another pair of legs.

More hooves thudded. That his skull wasn't caved in was a wonder.

He heaved upright but was only halfway when two horses came together---with him caught between them. His chest and back flared with pain. For harrowing moments he thought his ribs were shattered but when the horses pranced away he seemed to be intact.

His nephew's animal bolted.

Darting forward, Sapariche lunged at his own.

There was a terrible squeal.

The grizzly was attacking the pack horse. The bear's jaws closed on its neck and its claws raked deep as the horse sought to break free.

Sapariche had his own hide to think of. He grabbed the tether to his animal and yanked. The stake came out easy and he got a grip to climb on. Or tried to. His horse shied, causing him to lose his footing. Clinging fast, he was half dragged.

Sapariche locked his fingers in the animal's mane and swung his leg up. But the horse chose that instant to buck, and the next Sapariche knew, he was hanging by one arm and a leg.

The horse fled into the night.

"No!" Sapariche cried, but he was wasting his

breath. He bounced and flounced and very nearly lost his hold. "Stop!"

His horse was too overcome with fright to heed. In utter terror it galloped down a wood-covered slope.

All it would take was for a log or boulder to loom out of the darkness and disaster would result.

Sapariche desperately tried to climb on. He got his other arm up and was about to leverage his body higher when he saw a tree appear out of nowhere. His horse tried to swerve to avoid it.

And failed.

Sapariche felt a jarring blow to his head and shoulders and then he was tumbling into a nothingness as black as a starless night.

Chapter 8

Nate King was up before anyone else. At his request the settlers had kept someone on watch all night, in shifts. Jacob had the last shift, and Nate wasn't the least bit surprised to see the youth sitting up but sound asleep by the fire.

Rising carefully so as not to awaken Winona, Nate took his Hawken and moved to where he had a magnificent view of the first rays of sunshine bursting above the eastern horizon. The plains and foothills were yet mired in shadow.

Sunrise was one of his favorite times of day. Watching the sun come up was a promise of new experiences to come. A promise, in its way, of life itself.

Nate grinned at the turns his mind took. Ever since he could remember, he'd possessed what others might call a philosophical bent. He often wondered about the why and the wherefore of it all. Which explained the bookshelf in his cabin with more books than just about anyone west of the Mississippi River.

Nate stretched and turned to see if Jacob was still asleep---and nearly bumped into Clara Gordon. The girl was bundled in a blanket and her hair was dishevelled from sleep. "Morning, little one," he said in amusement. It was rare for anyone to come up on him unnoticed.

"Good morning Mr. King," Clara said politely. She stepped up beside him and gazed out over the predawn world. "Did you see the bear?"

"Can't see much of anything yet," Nate said.

"My pa says I'm being foolish worrying about it," Clara said. She looked up at him. "Do you think I'm being foolish?"

"It didn't attack any of you," Nate said. "It wandered off and is probably miles away by now."

Clara shook her head. "No."

Nate didn't blame the girl for being afraid. Grizzlies scared him, too. "You're that sure?"

"I dreamed about it again," Clara said. "That makes two nights in a row."

"Some folks take dreams as omen but they don't alway mean something. I've had a lot of dreams that were just, well, dreams," Nate said. Curious, he asked, "What was yours about?"

Clara tucked her chin into her blanket and said so softly he could barely hear her, "It killed us. All of us. In my dream I screamed and screamed but there was nothing I could do."

"The dream was the same both nights?"

Clara nodded.

Again, Nate told himself that fear was to blame. Then again, Winona placed great credence in her own dreams. It prompted him to inquire, "Where did all this happen?"

"Somewhere I've never been. A place with a lot of grass and a stream."

"That could be anywhere," Nate said. The mountains were full of valleys and waterways.

"There was a tree," Clara said.

"Eh?"

"A big dead tree in both of my dreams," Clara said. "It didn't have any leaves or anything. Most of the top was black."

"Trees struck by lightning often look like that," Nate mentioned.

"I never saw one before," Clara said. "But it was so real in my dream. There were black birds sitting on the branches. They were like crows only bigger."

"Ravens," Nate guessed.

"The bear came from behind the dead tree and....," Clara stopped and bent her chin lower. "It was awful."

"No need to talk about it," Nate said.

"I'm glad you're with us, Mr. King," Clara said. "You and Mrs. King, both. I feel safer." She turned. "Well, I better get back with my mother. She'll be upset if she wakes up and finds I wandered off." The girl headed for the wagons but paused to say, "Be on the lookout for that bear, will you?"

"You can bet I will, be" Nate said.

Sapariche became aware of a breeze on his face and heard the distant cry of a fox. Confused, he struggled to remember where he was and why he was apparently lying on rocky ground.

Suddenly everything came back in a rush. The grizzly. His brother and his nephew. The horses fleeing. Him, trying to climb on and being slammed against a tree.

He opened his eyes and had to squint against the bright glare. He was facing east and the sun was well into the sky. Half the morning had gone by.

Sapariche went to rise and wished he hadn't. Pain flared from his hip to his shoulder. His ribs, in particular, were terribly sore. He worried something was broken. But he could move his arm well enough, and when he sat up and probed, he was pleased to discover that while he was battered and bruised, his bones appeared to be intact.

His horse was long gone. He supposed he shouldn't be mad. A bear like that would scare anything.

The bear!

Sapariche twisted and stared up the slope. There was no sign of it. He was surprised, and grateful, it hadn't come after him.

Sapariche slowly stood. His knife was still in its sheath. It wouldn't be of much use against a grizzly but it was the only weapon he had.

Part of him wanted to run away. Part of him knew beyond any doubt that Tishawat and Ungamo were dead and the prudent thing to do was get out of there while he still could.

The grizzly might be lurking nearby.

Instead, Sapariche drew his knife and warily climbed toward their camp.

He was a warrior.

He would act as one.

He would see to it that whatever remained of his brother and nephew were buried so that scavengers did not get at them.

He would reclaim his lance.

And perhaps, just perhaps, one of the horses had returned.

STALKED

Sapariche took his time. His ribs ached abominably. It hurt just to breathe. Plus, there was the threat of the bear.

The woods were ominously still. Not so much as the chirp of a bird broke the quiet.

He smelled a vestige of smoke from their fire, which had long since gone out, and came around a pine and there was their camp.

Sapariche stopped short, stunned.

It was a ruin. A complete, total, utter ruin. An act of wanton destruction worse than the whirlwinds that came down out of the sky and sucked up lodges and people, alike.

The bear had destroyed everything. Every weapon. Every parfleche. Every strip of clothing. The bodies, the parts not consumed, were scattered amid the wreckage of their bows and quivers and the lance. The bear hadn't been satisfied with ripping and breaking. No. The grizzly tore it all to bits and pieces. Every last item.

Sapariche could hardly credit his senses. He never heard of a such a thing. Bears could be destructive, yes. But never like this. It spoke of a viciousness that went beyond mere savagery.

This was more than a grizzly on a rampage. This was a beast gone mad.

Sapariche moved through the debris. There lay a broken arrow. Beside it, a jagged strip of leather from a strap. Beside that, a tooth. He spied part of a jawbone speckled with flesh, a severed hand, the fingers gnawed partially off. Other body parts were strewn here and there.

Sapariche bowed his chin and closed his eyes. He was shaken to his core.

This was horror beyond horror.

He opened his eyes and beheld other eyes staring back at him. It was Ungamo. Or, to be exact, Ungamo's head. Inexplicably, the grizzly left it intact. It sat there in the grass, Ungamo's face reflecting the shock Ungamo felt at the moment of his terrible death. the mouth was agape, the tongue visible, the teeth red from spilled blood.

"Nephew," Sapariche said sadly. He cast about and saw Tishawat's head further off. Unlike Ungamo's, most of Tishawat's face and hair were gone. His skull had been split open and the brains scooped out. Or possibly licked out.

Misery brought Sapariche to his knees. His eyes moistened and a lump formed in his throat. To lose two of the people he loved most in so hideous a fashion was almost too much to endure.

Dizziness assailed him. Sapariche placed a hand on the ground to keep from collapsing. In doing so he almost touched a severed toe.

Never in all his winters had he come across a hint of anything like this.

He tried to make sense of it. Had they angered the bear somehow? Had they inadvertently done something to arouse such rage? Not that he knew of.

The slaughter, the destruction, might seem random. And yet, Sapariche sensed there was more to it.

He sensed that this bear was different.

People encountered grizzlies all the time. Usually

the people went one way and the grizzly went another.

Attacks happened, but they were no more common than being bit by a rattlesnake. When they had occurred, no grizzly ever did as this one had done.

He found a clear paw print in a pool of blood and marveled at the size. The claws were half as long as his knife.

Sapariche roved in search of other sign. He discovered where the grizzly had crept out of the forest to take Ungamo by surprise. Long had he heard that grizzlies were capable of great stealth. That when they wanted to, they could move as silently as a cat.

He searched some more and came on partial prints that showed the direction the bear took when it left.

West.

Due west.

Toward the mountains.

"Good," Sapariche said aloud. The grizzly was gone and he could put his mind to other matters. Such as whether he should continue on to Bent's Fort or return to his village. Either, on foot, would take many days.

He was debating which to do when he glanced at the tracks and realized something.

The settlers had been going west, too. Toward the very same mountains.

No, Sapariche thought, and grunted. It couldn't be. That the grizzly had gone in the same direction was a coincidence. Nothing more.

Or was it?

He surveyed the debris and the body parts and the blood and was unsure.

It could be the bear was following the whites.

It could be that the grizzly had been on their trail when he and his brother and nephew blundered upon it.

The bear had kept out of sight and patiently bided its time and when two of them were asleep and Ungamo was by the fire, the bear snuck out of the darkness to wreak havoc.

Which begged a question.

Was the grizzly's intention to do the same to the settlers? Was it stalking them much like a cougar would stalk a deer or wolves stalked their prey?

He remembered the little girl and boy and was reminded of his own children when they were that young. He would hate for them to suffer the same grisly fate as Tishawat and Ungamo.

Sapariche came to a decision. He was not going on to Bent's Fort. Nor was he returning to his village.

Against all better judgement, against all common sense, Sapariche placed his hand on the hilt of his knife and headed west.

He must warn the settlers.

Chapter 9

Clara liked Mr. and Mrs. King.

Mr. King was bigger and looked stronger than her pa. She felt safer with him around.

Mrs. King fascinated her. She never knew an Indian before. The stories she had heard, she imagined they hated whites, even the womenfolk. But Mrs. King was as nice as could be. Always smiling at her, and always so polite.

Their daughter was another matter. Bright Rainbow kept to herself. She hung back all the time. During suppertime, too, she hardly ever said a word. Since Bright Rainbow was older than her, Clara figured she and Alice might strike up a friendship. But no. Alice wouldn't have anything to do with her. When Clara asked Alice why, her sister said she had tried to talk to Bright Rainbow a couple of times and Bright Rainbow seemed uncomfortable about it.

"Maybe she doesn't like whites," Alice said.

"Could be she's just shy."

Clara was determined to learn more about the girl. So, on the third day that the Kings were with them, with Nate King up ahead leading them toward a valley he knew of that might suit her pa, Clara made it a point to drop back until she was walking beside Bright Rainbow's horse.

The Indian girl looked down. She didn't say anything. Didn't smile, neither.

"Nice day," Clara said.

Bright Rainbow stared straight ahead.

"In case no one has told you, I'm Clara."

The Indian girl went on staring.

"You're Bright Rainbow," Clara said. "Sure is a pretty name. I like rainbows. Do you?"

Bright Rainbow's eyes flicked toward her.

"Look, I'm younger than you," Clara said. "But that doesn't mean we can't be friends. I'd like to get to know you better but you're awful hard to talk to." Clara had a thought that made her jerk her head up. "Wait a minute. What a dunce I am. I bet you don't talk because you don't speak our language. Do you know any?"

Clara waited, and when no answer was forthcoming, she started to get mad. Then it hit her. She slapped her forehead and laughed. "Of course you can't say you don't if you can't speak it!"

Bright Rainbow did something Clara hadn't seen her do before. She grinned. "I speak little bit. Speak Shoshone more."

Clara squealed in delight. "So we can talk! That means we can be friends, you and me."

Bright Rainbow didn't respond.

"Don't stop talking already," Clara said. "Tell me about yourself and I'll tell you about me. No. Wait. I'll go first to break the ice, then you can." Clara cleared her throat. "Let's see. I'm from South Carolina. That's a place in the South. We lived in the nicest hills you ever did see. Had a nice cabin and plenty of land. But my pa wasn't happy. Too many new folks were moving in so he reckoned as how he would pull up stakes and head for the Rockies." She paused to catch a breath. "And here we are."

"You want come?" Bright Rainbow asked.

Clara made sure her pa and ma were far enough ahead that they wouldn't hear her. "Not really, no. I liked it there. We had kin and friends. I was happy." She sighed and gazed at the high peaks and tiered slopes far above. "I don't know if I'll be as happy here. I already don't like it much. It's too scary."

"Scary?" Bright Rainbow said.

"Bears and the like," Clara said. "I saw a huge one that about made me wet myself. There's other dangers, too. A lot of them from what I hear."

"Many dangers," Bright Rainbow said.

"So you understand?"

Bright Rainbow's face clouded. "Understand good. My mother, my father, killed by mountain lion."

Clara nearly tripped over her own feet, she was so surprised. "Mr. and Mrs. King aren't your real folks?"

Bright Rainbow shook her head. "Winona like me. She take me for hers."

"I had no idea," Clara said. "I'm sorry that you lost your ma and pa. You're lucky that nice people like the Kings took you in. I knew a girl back to home, her ma and pa were killed in a fire and she had to go live in an orphanage in the city. We visited her once and, oh my, she hated it. She hugged me and cried and cried and said as how she wished her folks were still alive."

"I wish too," Bright Rainbow said sadly.

"I reckon I'm the lucky one," Clara said. "Still having mine."

"Brother and sister too."

"I suppose I should be grateful for them, too," Clara said. "But they treat me like a kid all the time and I don't like that much."

"Kings have son. Name Zach. Him much older. Married." Bright Rainbow paused. "They have daughter too. Her name Evelyn. She has husband now."

"I guess you and me will have one too some day," Clara said, and chuckled. "But between you and me, I don't see where boys are anything to crow about. I'd as soon have a kitten as a husband."

Bright Rainbow laughed.

Clara was proud of herself. She had gotten the girl to loosen up. "Once we're settled in, I hope you can come visit now and then. It will just be us and the Walberg's. Gunther is all right but he's not a girl."

"He look away when I come near."

Clara giggled. "He's shy, is all. His big brother, Hermann, is friendly."

"Your brother shy?"

"Jacob?" Clara snorted. "Not that I ever saw. To be honest. he's a little pushy at times."

"Him have nice face. Handsome, whites call it."

Startled, Clara glanced up. "Jacob? Are you feeling poorly? Or is that you need spectacles?"

"Spectacles?"

"Eyeglasses." Clara held her fingers to her eyes as if she were wearing a pair. "So you can see better."

Bright Rainbow giggled.

"Jacob is as ordinary as rocks," Clara said, and had another thought. "Hold on. You haven't taken a shine to him, have you?"

"Shine?"

"You're not in love with him or anything, are you?"

Bright Rainbow blushed. "No. All I say is him handsome."

"Mrs. King should check your forehead and see if you have a fever," Clara joked.

"I like you," Bright Rainbow said. "We be friends."

"Can't ever have enough of those," Clara said.

Sapariche wasn't as spry as he used to be. Becoming old did that. A person became slower. Less agile. Their reflexes weren't as swift as they once were. He should know. He had gone through all of it. Not to a great degree yet. Not to where he would spend his days sitting in his lodge. In another ten winters or so, perhaps.

As it was, by the time the sun had arced midway across the sky, he was tired and his knees hurt. It was the climbing.

The bear was easy enough to follow. Not that grizzlies always left a lot of sign. But this one wasn't making any effort to hide it's passage. It was moving fast, too. Faster than grizzlies usually did.

Sapariche wondered if perhaps the bear was eager to catch up to the whites.

His own eagerness drove him on. With their help, with their guns, he could slay the bear. He would avenge his brother and nephew. And go back to his people with a token of his triumph, namely, the grizzly's hide.

Sapariche considered resting and decided against it.

He would forge on for as long as he could. He needed to stay close to the grizzly. Not *too* close. Enough that when they caught up to the whites, he could slip around the bear and appraise them of their peril.

Yet another slope rose before him.

Sapariche was breathing heavily when he came to the top and stopped to catch his breath. He was relieved to see a broad meadow partially ringed by trees. About to start across, he suddenly stopped cold and crouched.

Across the meadow something had moved. Something large in the shadow of tall pines.

The grizzly! Sapariche thought, and gripped his knife. Not that it would be of much use should the bear attack. A knife against a grizzly was ludicrous. He might as well throw pebbles.

There was the movement again.

The undergrowth parted and out stepped a horse.

Sapariche's pulse quickened. He recognized the animal. It was Ungamo's stallion. Apparently it was heading for their village but taking its sweet time or it would have gone farther by now. It came into the open, lowered its head, and nipped at the grass.

Sapariche smiled. The animal knew him. Knew his scent. All he had to do was slowly approach and speak soothingly and it would let him mount.

Sapariche was rising when more movement caused him to freeze.

Something else was in those pines.

Something as big as the horse.

A huge head appeared behind it.

Hungrily grazing, the stallion didn't notice.

Sapariche fought down an urge to shout a warning.

STALKED

It might save the stallion, although over short distances grizzlies were reputed to be even faster than horses. But the bear would know he was there and might come after him, instead.

Moving stealthily, the grizzly emerged. It wasn't more than the lengths of three canoes from the stallion but the horse was oblivious.

Sapariche held his breath. Inwardly, he willed the stallion to look up. To run.

The bear crept closer, ever closer, and despite its size, despite its sheer bulk, it must be making no sounds whatsoever.

Suddenly the stallion raised its head.

Sapariche saw the bear halt in the act of lifting a forepaw.

The stallion looked to either side but not behind it. Giving its head a toss, it flicked its tail and resumed eating.

Sapariche changed his mind. He must do something. He couldn't let the stallion be slain without at least trying to help. Dropping flat, he cupped his hands to his mouth close to the ground and let out with a howl worthy of a wolf.

The stallion's head swept up, its ears pricked, and it took a couple of steps.

At that very instant that the grizzly attacked. A sweep of a forepaw caught the horse a raking blow across the hindquarters.

The stallion squealed and bolted and the grizzly pounded in pursuit.

Sapariche beheld proof of the claim that grizzlies were swifter than a horse. In what seemed like mere heartbeats the bear was abreast of the stallion and bit at its leg. The stallion swerved and ran faster, its mane and tail flying.

The grizzly ran faster, too.

They were halfway across the meadow when the bear flung itself at its prey and slammed into the horse with the force of an avalanche. The stallion stumbled and nearly went down. It recovered but by then the grizzly's jaw were gnashing at its neck. The stallion kicked, and Sapariche heard the thuds clear from where he lay.

The horse didn't stand and fight. It wisely fled again.

The grizzly came after it.

Belatedly, Sapariche realized that the chase was bringing them directly toward him.

Chapter 10

Nate King was troubled. He had offered to lead the two families to an ideal spot to settle. But the more he got to know them, the less sure he was that they could make a go of it.

They had the right spirit, if not much else. Well, some of them. Charles was the most eager. Jacob, taking his cue from his father, was also excited about starting anew. Elizabeth, Nate suspected, wasn't as enthusiastic. She was doing it because her husband wanted to do it. Alice, their oldest girl, didn't seem to care much one way or the other. She was going along with it because she had no choice. Young Clara didn't like being there at all.

As for the other family, Otto Walberg didn't hide his reservations. From what Nate gathered, Otto had let Charles persuade him into coming along, and might be having regrets. Freida Walberg hid her feelings so well that Nate couldn't tell much except that she was one of those wives who stuck by their husband through thick and thin. Hermann was like Jacob. He looked up to his father and did whatever his father asked of him. Young Gunther, like Clara, liked being in the mountains least.

The crux of the issues was that even though the parents were willing, it didn't mean they were able.

They literally had no idea what they were in for.

When Nate mentioned the likelihood of encountering hostiles, Charles patted his rifle and said he was confident he could protect his loved ones. When Nate brought up how harsh the winters were, Charles declared that they would salt enough meat and make enough preserves to see them through the lean times.

Secretly, Nate worried that Charles Gordon might be more than a little bit of a fool.

Then again, Nate hadn't known what to expect when he first came to the Rocky Mountains, either. He had been young and cocksure and confident he could deal with whatever life threw at him.

It was unfortunate, Nate reflected, that wisdom usually came with age. The young thought they knew it all and actually knew very little.

The clomp of hooves coming alongside his bay put an end to his reverie.

"You are very deep in thought, husband," Winona remarked.

"I can't help feeling I'm making a mistake," Nate admitted. He was going to elaborate but he didn't need to. She knew him as well as he knew himself. Maybe better.

"If it is a mistake, it is their mistake, not yours," Winona said.

"If?"

"They might learn to survive. Others have."

"Could be," Nate acknowledged.

"You are looking at the dark side," Winona said. "Which is not like you."

"It's the little girl," Nate said.

"She is sweet, that one. She is getting along fine with our new daughter."

Nate glanced over his shoulder at Clara and Bright Rainbow, walking side by side, Bright Rainbow leading her horse by the reins. "I still can't quite think of her that way."

"Because we adopted her?"

"She had parents before us. And she was twelve when we took her in."

"But now she is ours," Winona said. "We must always treat her as such. Always show her the love that true parents show."

"I was just saying."

"Hmmph," Winona said.

"What does that mean?"

Winona grinned. "Just hmmph."

Nate surveyed the spectacular vista that surrounded them. To the north and south rolling hills were draped in the emerald and brown hues of forest. Due west reared titans of rock and earth, a few capped with sprinkles of white even at that time of year.

Miles high, the mountains were a testament to the splendor of creation.

On a cliff miles above, pale specks moved. Mountain sheep, Nate knew. In a meadow lower down, large animals grazed. By their size they must be elk. He was tempted to take out his spyglass but just then Jacob came running up.

"Mr King!"

Nate rested his Hawken across his saddle and turned. "What has you worked up?"

Jacob pointed at a stand of aspen about a hundred

yards away. "I think I saw a wolf."

"You might well have," Nate said. "There are a lot of them in the mountains."

Jacob hefted his rifle. "What do we do?"

"Nothing."

"But it's a wolf!" Jacob exclaimed. "Shouldn't we go after it? Hunt it down?"

"What for? It has as much right to breathe as you do."

Jacob's confusion was almost comical. "But wolves are dangerous. Everybody knows that. It's why they were all killed off in our neck of the country. Heck, all over back East. There's hardly a wolf left anywhere."

"Not many cougars, either," Nate said. "Bears are fewer each year too."

"What are you saying?"

Nate sighed. "Jacob, my son had a pet wolf for years. It stayed with us when it wanted to and went its way when it wanted to and never harmed any of us."

Jacob ran a hand through his tousled hair. "I still don't understand. That was one wolf. Other wolves might eat us given half a chance."

Nate reminded himself that the youth had been raised to believe that any creature that might prey on humans was to be exterminated. He'd thought the same way once. "I can count the number of wolf attacks I know of on one hand."

"Do we kill all because of a few?" Winona chimed in. "People kill, too. Do we wipe ourselves out to stop the killing?"

"That's plumb ridiculous," Jacob said.

"No more so than killing every wolf we see," Nate

said. "So no, we're not going to hunt the wolf down. If you see it again, though, let me know."

Jacob gnawed on his bottom lip, his brow furrowed. "When do you kill, then?"

"For the supper pot," Nate said. "Or when something is out to kill me or hurt those I care for. Otherwise, I let the wildlife be if they let me be."

"My pa shot a black bear once," Jacob said. "Back when I was eight. Him and other hunters brought it home hanging from a pole. He was real proud of himself. We had meat for months. I thought it was a great thing."

"He was providing for his family," Nate said. "You'll need to help him do that out here."

Jacob gazed at the distant peaks with obvious trepidation. "I hope I'm up to it." He turned on a heel to rejoin his family. "Anyway, I'll let you know if the wolf shows up again."

"Nice young man," Winona said.

"He's trying."

"I like that they are all so well-mannered."

Nate didn't say what he was thinking. That manners were fine but they didn't help much when a beast or hostile was out to do you in.

Sapariche didn't know if either animal had seen him. He hoped not. The stallion might seek his help but there was nothing he could do armed with a knife. The grizzly would seek to rend him to pieces.

Staying flat, Sapariche crawled toward a patch of brush. He needed to get under cover before the bear spotted him.

Out in the meadow, the grizzly nipped at the stallion's leg.

Blood sprayed and the horse neighed but keep fleeing at a gallop.

They were close now.

Sapariche swore he could feel the ground under him shake to the pounding of the stallion's heavy hooves. He reached the brush and parted it and slid from view, turning as he did to witness the outcome.

The grizzly was pacing its quarry. Running right beside the stallion and looking at it. Almost as if the grizzly were playing a game. Letting the horse think it could get away when it couldn't. Or maybe the bear was waiting for the right moment to strike.

That moment came.

The grizzly lunged, its teeth tearing into the stallion's belly. Not deep enough to eviscerate it but the stallion came to a sudden stop. Wheeling, the stallion went at the bear with its own teeth and its front hooves, biting and kicking in a frenzy the likes of which Sapariche never beheld in a horse.

Its forepaws flashing, the grizzly fought just as furiously.

Spinning, kicking, swinging, biting, the pair turned round and round, the neighs of the stallion and the roars of the grizzly mingling in a cacophony of combat.

Grass flew from under their paws and hoofs. Dust rose. And on they battled.

Sapariche marveled that the stallion was holding its own for as long as it had.

Then the horse clamped its teeth down on the bear's shoulder and the grizzly reacted by rearing onto its hind legs and delivering a blow that sent the stallion staggering.

Both creatures became still, glaring at one another, the stallion with its sides heaving from its exertions, blood smeared over its neck and sides and flank. Its every breath sounded like wind shearing through a narrow ravine. One of its legs would not stop twitching.

By contrast, the grizzly was as composed as if it had just emerged from a cave after hibernation. A few flecks of blood and a red streak on its shoulder were the only marks of their battle. It breathed easily, normally. And then it did an astonishing thing.

A cold ripple ran down Sapariche's spine as the grizzly flicked out its tongue and licked its lips. Just as a person would do when about to eat a delicious meal.

An act so vicious, so wicked, as to almost be human.

Sapariche knew he should turn and crawl away while he still could. But he stayed where he was. He couldn't help himself. He had to see the end. Even if it put him in heightened danger.

It seemed that the horse and bear stared at one another for an eternity. The bear was in no hurry and the horse was seeking to regain its strength.

The stallion broke the stand-off. It snapped at the grizzly and the grizzly stepped back to drop onto all fours.

Now it was the stallion that reared. Towering high, it flailed at the bear with hooves that could crush a skull. Some of the blows landed, too.

Sapariche clearly heard the thuds.

The bear twisted aside, swung a paw, but missed. The stallion came down and reared again. Its legs were clubs, its hooves rocks. The grizzly sidestepped and the stallion turned with it, relentless in its effort to drive the bear off or kill it.

Sapariche hoped the horse would succeed but the next instant his hope was crushed.

The grizzly's maw gaped wide and almost too quick for the human eyes to follow, its jaws clamped onto a foreleg. There was the crunch of bone and the horse squealed.

The grizzly let go, its mouth rimmed scarlet, and stood there as the horse dropped onto all fours, or tried to. Its foreleg was shattered, the white of bone gleaming bright. Unable to place its full weight on the hurt limb, it sought to limp away.

The grizzly let it. For all of eight to ten steps. Then the bear exploded into motion. Head low, hump hunched, it slammed into the stallion with such force, the horse was upended.

The end wasn't swift. It was slow and brutal. The bear did to the horse as it had done to Sapariche's brother and nephew. It ripped the stallion to chunks and pieces, not stopping until there was nothing recognizable except the skull and parts of the spine and other broken bones.

Sapariche thought he knew fear. He thought he could never be more scared than the other night.

He was wrong.

A realization had come over him.

This grizzly was evil.

Chapter 11

The valley was a green haven surrounded on three sides by peaks that reached to the clouds. From out of the heights flowed a stream that ran year-round and kept the grass green and the trees from withering even in the worst heat of the summer.

The stream was the main reason Nate thought the valley would be ideal for the settlers. Plus, the valley wasn't far in, which gave them easy access to the prairie and to buffalo. In addition, it was small, not quite half a mile in length and a quarter of a mile wide.

To Nate's knowledge, the tribes in the region had paid it few if any visits. It was out of the way. Perfect for two families who wanted to keep to themselves.

He knew of it because, decades ago, he and Shakespeare McNair had paid it a brief visit while searching for beaver.

The settlers were pleased as could be.

The adults walked around admiring the scenery while the younger ones, including Bright Rainbow, ran about exploring.

"You picked wisely, husband," Winona said as they sat watching the others. "They will be safer here than they would be most anywhere else."

Charles and Elizabeth Gordon came toward them, Charles all smiles.

"Mr. and Mrs. King, we can't thank you enough! This is exactly what we were looking for!"

"We are happy we could help," Winona said.

"There's still plenty of daylight left," Charles said. "You're not planning to leave right away are you?"

"We will stay the night," Winona said, and turned to Nate. "Unless you wanted to head out?"

"I've been thinking of sticking around a couple of days," Nate revealed. To do all he could for them, even if it was mainly offer advice on how to live longer.

"Good!" Charles exclaimed. "Then you can take part in the celebration!"

"For?" Nate said.

"Isn't it obvious?" Charles motioned at the valley. "Our new home! All thanks to you two!"

"I'm fixing to bake a cake," Elizabeth said. "And Otto lugged his ophicleide all the way from Pennsylvania so we'll have music."

"Ophicleide?" Nate said. He couldn't recollect ever hearing the word before.

"A musical instrument," Elizabeth said. "They were invented, oh, about twenty years ago. Probably after you came to the mountains, based on what you told us."

"You've probably missed out on a lot of new things" Charles said.

Nate gazed fondly at Winona. "I have all I need right here."

"Oh husband," Winona said, smiling. She reached over and took his hand.

Elizabeth clasped her own hands and grinned. "So much to do! If you care to help, Mrs. King, we'd be delighted."

"Or course," Winona said.

"I have wood to chop for our fire tonight," Charles said, hastening away.

Nate was about to go help when he spied Bright Rainbow, Clara and Gunther making toward the mouth of the valley. They were following the stream and were already well along. Not one had a weapon.

Cradling his Hawken, Nate strolled after them. They needed to learn that going anywhere in the wilds without a means to protect themselves was folly.

When his daughter Evelyn was young, time and again he had to impress on her how dangerous it was to go abroad unarmed. Eventually it sank in, to where these days she always had her rifle with her.

His son hadn't needed any persuasion. Zach took to guns like a fish to water.

Nate missed those years when they were little. Life was simpler. They were forever doings things that exasperated him but was part of their growing up.

Bright Rainbow and her new friends were climbing a grass-covered hillock that gave a good view of the way into the valley. On reaching the top they stood staring intently down the stream.

Nate made no sound as he approached. Not on purpose. Moving silently was second nature to him.

In the wilds stealth made for a longer life.

".....might be we are shed of it," Clara was saying. "But somehow I doubt it."

"We have come a long way," Gunther said.

"I think you safe now," Bright Rainbow said in her broken English.

"Safe from what?" Nate said. As if he had to ask.

Clara and Gunther jumped.

"Mr. King!" the girl declared. "You shouldn't sneak up on us like that!"

"I wasn't," Nate said. "You need to stay more alert." He gazed toward the foothills. "Let me guess what you hope you're safe from."

"The bear," Clara said.

"Still afraid it will show up?"

Clara nodded. "I feel it in my bones. I feel it as strong as I feel anything."

"You're just a girl," Gunther said.

"And you're just a boy," Clara said. "What does that prove?"

"We're not adults yet," Gunther said. "We don't know enough to be sure."

"Not sure is not good," Bright Rainbow said.

"How so?" Nate said to encourage her to go on. They were teaching her English but it was slow going. She could use more practice. Unlike Winona, who picked up new tongues like there was nothing to it, Bright Rainbow was struggling.

Nate struggled with new tongues, too. So he knew what she was going through. He also sensed a certain reluctance on her part. Since all three of them spoke Shoshone---and so did Evelyn and Zach, for that matter---why bother learning the white tongue?

"Animals kill," Bright Rainbow said, her features marked by sorrow.

Nate knew she was thinking of her mother and father and the mountain lion that slew them. It was rare for the big cats to attack humans, but not unknown. "I agree. Never take an animal lightly."

"I'm not," Clara said. "My dream warned me and I believe my dream."

"Sometimes dreams are just dreams, remember?" Nate reminded her. "But we'll keep our eyes skinned. Just in case."

"Please do," Clara said.

Sapariche stared at what was left of the stallion, and shuddered. It was as if the horse had been chopped apart by fifty tomahawks.

The grizzly had ripped and torn and bit until whatever drove it was satiated.

Sapariche stayed hidden until the bear was well gone. Only when he saw it cross the crest of a hill in the distance higher up did he rise and shake his leg to relieve a cramp and come to study the aftermath.

The question Sapariche would very much like to answer was 'why'? Why did the grizzly kill so viciously? Why reduce its prey to....this?

Over the many winters of his life Saparice had heard of predators gone berserk. A cornered wolverine. A wolf in a frenzy. One of the big tawny cats in the grip of bloodlust.

This was different.

This was like nothing in his experience.

This was why he was beginning to believe the bear was evil.

His people had long known of evil's existence. When a mother gave birth, she would put the umbilical cord on an ant hill to ward off evil spirits. Skinwalkers were especially feared for their evil natures. They were known to shapeshift into all kinds of animals. Coyotes.

Foxes. Wolves. Birds. Even bears.

Sapariche wondered if the grizzly might perhaps be a skinwalker. They delighted in inflicting harm. His cousin once told him about a skinwalker who changed into a coyote and stole a baby right out of a cradleboard with the mother not an arm's length away.

But Sapariche had never heard of a skinwalker doing what this grizzly was doing. It was as if the bear lived to destroy. Not merely to fill its belly.

This grizzly killed for the sole sake of killing. Not swiftly. Not efficiently. This one took its time. This one ripped flesh down to the bone, then broke and shattered the bone.

Another possibility occurred to him.

He remembered a horse belonging to an uncle. A good horse with a peaceful temperament. One day it was kicked in the head by another horse and after that no one could go near it or it would try to stomp them into the ground. His uncle put the horse under.

Could this grizzly have suffered a blow to the head, like that horse??

Sapariche shook himself. So many questions. He turned to go and took a few steps and looked up and stopped cold.

The smell of blood and gore was strong. So strong, the breeze had undoubtedly wafted it far and wide.

A smell that would lure meat-eaters like honey drew bears. And did.

Two wolves had come out of the trees to the south and were staring at him.

Sapariche straightened and put his hand on his knife. Wolves seldom attacked people. But seldom was not never. He kept going but held to a walk. To show fear, to run, might provoke an attack.

The wolves glanced at one another and padded toward him.

How he would love to have a lance or a bow, Sapariche thought. Or a horse. He was so accustomed to riding everywhere, he had forgotten how vulnerable someone on foot could be.

Compared to other creatures in the wild, people were easy prey. Unless they were armed, they were no match for teeth and claws and stronger sinews.

Sapariche stopped and faced the wolves. If their intent was to harm him, let them try when he was ready for them.

The pair came on until they were close enough that he could see the amber of the male's eyes and the brown of the female's. They were in their prime, their fur as lustrous as a woman's freshly washed hair.

They stared at him and Sapariche stared back.

When all they did was go on staring, Sapariche cleared his throat. "Peace to you, brother and sister. I mean you no harm and hope you mean me none. I am after a bear, the enemy of your kind. If you will let me be on my way, I will sing a song to you when I return to my people."

The male raised its long nose to the breeze and the black tip twitched. It looked at the female and somehow she understood what the male was thinking and they turned as one and moved toward the swath of blood and flesh.

"May your winters be many," Sapariche called after them and bent his steps to the west.

He didn't look back until he reached the other side of the meadow.

The wolves were licking at the remains as eagerly as Ute children would lick the sweet sap of a box elder tree after the sap was boiled.

Sapariche hiked on. He put his mind to his eventual confrontation with the bear. The white settlers might not be of much help, after all, even with their rifles.

No. The best way to stop this particular grizzly....was to have Grizzly Killer kill it.

Chapter 12

Clara was feeling guilty. Everyone else had something to feel happy about. But not her.

Her pa and Mr. Walberg were as happy as could be about the valley. It had everything they wanted.

Her ma and Mrs. Walberg were happy, too. In a few shorts months they would both have new cabins to live in. Her ma couldn't wait, as she put it, to have "a real roof over our heads so we can be safe and warm'.

Jacob and Alice and Hermann and Gunther were happy their long journey was finally over.

Clara supposed she should be happy too. But as she had told Mr. King, she couldn't stop thinking about the bear.

It was strange.

She would be doing some chore her ma set for her or be running around with Gunther and Bright Rainbow and suddenly the image of the grizzly would pop into her head and she would worry that she was going to run into it again.

Her ma had always said that she fretted too much and maybe her ma was right.

"Just stop thinking about it!" was her mother's solution.

Clara tried. Each time she started thinking about the bear she would tell herself to stop. It didn't always work. More than half the time she went on fretting anyway.

Mr. King seemed to understand. When she talked to him about it, he didn't make light of it like her own folks did.

Now she needed to try harder than ever.

The campfire was crackling and lanterns had been hung and everyone was in fine spirits. They were putting on their best clothes and their mothers had made treats.

In a little while their celebration would commence.

"Now remember," her ma said while helping her into the finest dress she owned. They were in their wagon, changing. "No shenanigans tonight."

"Yes, ma," Clara said.

"Try not to get any food on your dress. Sometimes the stains won't come out."

"Yes, ma."

"And whatever you do, don't tear it like you're always doing with your workaday dress."

"Yes, ma."

"You have to learn to take better care of your clothes. It makes my job easier."

Clara was going to say 'Yes, ma' one more time but instead she sighed and nodded.

"And don't pout." Her ma cocked her head. "What ails you, anyhow? And don't tell me that stupid bear."

"I haven't thought about the bear all day," Clara fibbed.

Her ma gently took her by the shoulders and turned her so they were face to face. "Listen to me, little one. We're about to start a new life. It will be different than back home. Out here there are more wild animals and such but you can't spend every minute worrying about them or you'll be miserable. You don't want that, do you?"

"No." Clara surely didn't.

"Then shut that grizzly out of your head."

"I don't know how."

"It's easy. Listen." Her ma put an arm around her shoulders. "There have been a lot of times when I've had to shut things out. Bad things. Things I'd rather not remember. Whenever one of them tries to creep back into my head, I gave my head a shake and say in my head, "No!" And I refuse to let it bother me."

"I tried that."

"It takes practice," her ma said. "Keep trying. We can't control everything that goes on around us but we can control what goes on between our ears. If you don't like what your mind is doing, stop it."

"I'll work at it," Clara said.

"I know you will." Her ma kissed her on the cheek. "I know I don't say it enough, but you're a good girl, Clara. I'm proud of you. Proud of how you are. Alice can be contrary at times but you always do as we ask without much fuss. Your pa and I appreciate that."

Clara felt her cheeks grow warm.

"You'll like it here, little one," her ma said. "Once you've put that nasty old bear out of your head, you'll be as happy as can be."

"I sure hope so," Clara said.

When Nate King was a young man in New York he courted a woman named Adeline. She loved music and dancing and dragged him to every dance she could.

He didn't mind. Fact was, he liked getting out and meeting people. And after spending all day tied to his desk as an accountant, he liked the exercise.

Adeline's favorite was the country dance. Couples would take turns passing between a long line, holding each other's hand and dipping and turning.

Nate liked the Scotch reel because it was livelier.

They also danced the cotillion and the waltz, which was slow to catch on because it was considered too intimate and scandalous.

All this came to mind as he sat watching the settlers and their children having a grand time. They were singing and clapping and dancing, as carefree as could be.

Winona nudged him with her elbow and said, "We should join in, husband. Have fun."

Nate nodded in agreement and gazed past her at Bright Rainbow, who had not said much since the festivities began. "You too, daughter.," he said in Shoshone.

"No," Bright Rainbow said.

Winona showed her surprise. "Why not? I thought you like Clara and Gunther and the rest."

"Clara and Gunther," Bright Rainbow said. "The others treat me different."

"Different how?" Winona said.

"They do not like me."

"Have they been rude?" Nate asked.

"No. But I can tell."

"Perhaps you misjudge them," Winona said.

Nate had noticed that Jacob, Alice and Hermann

spent a lot of time together and tended to ignore the younger ones. Which was typical. But he'd never seen any of them look at Bright Rainbow as if they didn't care for her. He was going to question her when Charles Gordon gave a shout and the rest stopped what they were doing to listen.

"It's time for Otto to treat us to some music, as he promised!"

Nate was familiar with a lot of musical instruments. The violin, the cello, the lute, the harp, the piano, the dulcimer, and more. But he had never in his life heard of an ophicleide.

As instruments went, the thing was huge. Made of brass, it consisted mainly of a long tube, wide at one end and narrowing as it bent back and around, with a lot of keys and pads. If the brass were stretched out straight, it would be seven to eight feet long.

Apparently it had been in the Walberg family for years. Otto's father had taken it up, and later Otto, although he remarked that he hadn't played it in a long while and only kept it because it was his father's.

Making himself comfortable on a log, Otto proceeded to hold the thing so that the wide end pointed almost straight up, and then put his lips to the mouthpiece. He puffed a few times and worked a few keys and gave off sounds that made Nate think of geese honking.

Winona laughed merrily. Putting her hand on Nate's knee, she teased, "You whites never cease to amaze me."

"We amaze me too," Nate said.

"Whenever you're ready, Otto," Charles said.

Walberg coughed a few times and began to play.

Nate didn't know what to expect. He was familiar with trumpets and horns and bugles. But none matched the range of this strange new instrument. As he listened, he smiled at the incongruity of sitting there in the wilds with musical melodies wafting about.

"He plays well, does he not?" Winona said.

Nate nodded.

The Gordon family was enrapt.

Mrs. Walberg looked at her husband adoringly.

The ophicleide was loud. So loud, Nate almost didn't hear the nicker of his bay. He glanced toward their horses, which were tethered between the wagons, and saw that all three had their heads raised and were staring to the north.

Nate figured they had caught the scent of a prowling cougar or a passing wolf or coyote. Then he noticed their ears were pricked. They were listening. Listening intently. He turned his head and did the same but could hear nothing but the ophicleide.

Otto went on playing.

Nate tried to concentrate on the music but couldn't. The horses bothered him. The way they were standing told him that whatever they heard might pose a threat.

Winona leaned toward him so her lips were close to his ear. "Husband?"

Nate motioned at their mounts.

"What do you think it is?"

"Could be anything," Nate said. Which wasn't entirely true. Raccoons and foxes and the like wouldn't cause the horses any concern.

"With the fire and the noise, we are safe enough,"

Winona said.

Otto was so engrossed in the song, his eyes were closed and he tapped his feet as he played. The notes swelled, filling the night and echoing off the peaks.

Nate reckoned the sounds must carry for miles.

"The horses are still listening," Winona said.

"I'll be right back," Nate said. Easing into a crouch, he backed away so as not to disturb anyone else. Once he was in the clear, he stood. He went to the horses and listened but didn't hear anything to account for their behavior.

"What is it?" Nate said, giving his bay a couple of pats.

Just then one of the oxen uttered a loud snort and ponderously rose. Tossing its head, it stared in the same direction as the horses.

Still, Nate heard nothing. Not over the music and the clapping and the stomping of feet.

He moved further out to hear better, past a wagon's tongue into the open. Somewhere to the west a wolf howled. Much closer an owl hooted.

That was all.

He started to turn back and stopped. From out of the benighted forest to the north came crackling. Something was out there. Something big.

The crackling grew louder.

Suddenly an enormous bulk exploded out of the woods and bore down on their camp.

Chapter 13

Nearly everyone back in the States had heard of bison. Or buffalo, as they were more commonly called. Newspapers published many accounts of the enormous herds that roamed the plains. Numbering in the millions, they were a literal sight to behold.

But the plains buffalo weren't the only kind.

Hardly anyone knew there was a second type. The newspapers rarely mentioned them.

Far fewer in number, the other bison preferred forest over grassland. Woods bison, they were called.

Nate King and those like him in the Mountain Man fraternity alluded to them as mountain buffs.

Larger than their prairie cousins, with bigger humps that weren't quite as rounded, they lived in much smaller herds, often only a few dozen at the most, and were much more wary of humans.

They were also much more aggressive when provoked.

Whenever Nate encountered any, he made it a point to fight shy of them.

But now he didn't have a choice.

It was a woods bison that exploded out of the forest. A gigantic embodiment of sheer destruction, with curved horns that could rip a man or a horse asunder.

Nate was caught flat-footed. The buff was almost

on top of him within seconds. He didn't try to jerk his Hawken up and shoot. There wasn't time. All he could do was throw himself to one side.

He was in midair when the bison thundered past, so close that it brushed his shoulder.

"Look out!" he bawled. "Buffalo!"

It was a wonder anyone heard him, what with Otto playing and the rest laughing and clapping and dancing.

Little Clara did. She turned and pointed and screamed.

Bright Rainbow shouted.

Winona leaped to her feet, yelling.

The settlers were transfixed, but to their credit, only for the few moments it took the buff to loom in the firelight. In a mad confusion they scattered right and left.

Otto Walberg, intent on playing his ophicleide, didn't stop or look up. His instrument was too loud. Plus he was facing in the wrong direction.

Freida Walberg saved him. She saw that the buffalo was making right for him and hurled herself at her man. Knocking the ophicleide aside, she wrapped her other arm around Otto and bore both of them to the ground.

By then Nate was rising, his Hawken to his shoulder. He didn't shoot, though. He didn't have a clear shot at the bison's vitals.

The ophicleide toppled to the ground and gave off a few harsh notes.

Nate had witnessed some amazing things in his time but few could hold a candle to what happened next.

The bison lowered its head and slammed into the instrument as if trying to drive it into the earth. A flip of its head was evidently meant to toss the ophicleide as buffalo tossed wolves. But somehow the instrument became stuck to the buff's horn and the ophicleide flopped across the animal's face.

The bison went into a frenzy. It bucked and stomped and spun, all the while whipping its massive head about. That it didn't smash into one of the settlers was nothing less than a miracle.

"Stay out of its way!" Elizabeth shrieked.

Not heeding, Charles took a step in close but had to scramble back when the buffalo swung in his direction.

Somehow it missed him and crashed into the Gordon's wagon. Wood splintered and the canvas ripped but the wagon stayed upright.

Still trying to shake the ophicleide off, whipping right and left, the bison blundered into the campfire, scattering fireflies every which way.

Another bound, and the buffalo came toward Nate again. He darted aside but something struck him on the shins and he lost his balance and fell to his hands and knees.

When he looked up, the mountain buff was almost to the woods. With a loud snort it disappeared into the darkness.

Beside Nate lay the ophicleide. Or, rather, the mangled tangle of what had once been the musical pride and joy of the Walberg family. The wide end was crushed, the tubing twisted.

"Good God Almighty!" Charles Gordon exclaimed.

"What *was* that?" Elizabeth said, aghast.

All of them were slowly rising and shaking their

heads in disbelief or, in Alice's case, touching herself to make sure she wasn't hurt and beaming at her good fortune.

Nate went to Winona and Bright Rainbow. Neither had been harmed.

Winona said in astonishment, "Did you see, husband?"

"Who ever heard of the like?" Elizabeth said.

Otto and Freida were helping one another to stand.

"My father's ophicleide!" Otto said in dismay. "Why would that animal do such a thing?"

Gunther, usually so quiet, spoke up with, "It must not like music much."

Elizabeth and Alice started laughing.

"It's not funny!" Otto said angrily. "My instrument can never be replaced. All the joy it could have given us, and that animal destroyed it." He turned toward Nate. "Why? In heaven's name explain it to me."

"The sound, maybe," Nate said although he had no real idea.

"The low notes," Winona said. "Buffalo make a lot of sounds, Mr. Walberg. They grunt. They bellow. They roar, too, when the males fight over females."

"Are you suggesting that bison thought my ophicleide was another bison?" Otto said.

"That's preposterous," Freida said.

"It's the only thing I can think of," Winona said.

"At least it wasn't that awful grizzly," Clara said.

Elizabeth turned to her. "Stop with the bear talk. It's miles away by now. And grizzlies don't attack musical instruments. They attack people."

Charles laughed. "Bear or buffalo, the one thing I

know is that we were terribly lucky. Am I right, Mr. King, or am I right?"

"Right as rain," Nate said.

Sapariche first noticed the coyotes toward the middle of the morning when he stopped near the top of a steep slope to catch his breath.

It bothered him, how old he was feeling. His legs, in particular, were not as spry and tireless as they used to be. He also had an ache in his side.

Putting a hand to his ribs, he wished he were young again. As he had been when he only saw twenty winters. Then he never grew tired. Then he never had such awful aches.

Smiling at how silly he was being, Sapariche arched his back and stretched and glanced over his shoulder to be sure the pair of wolves hadn't followed him.

They hadn't.

But two coyotes were at the bottom of the slope, staring up at him.

Sapariche blinked.

They stood there as brazen as anything. A male and female. A big pair, but then coyotes in the mountains grew bigger than those lower down. Why, Sapariche couldn't say, but it was something he had seen with his own eyes so it was true.

Seeing a coyote always reminded Sapariche of the Trickster. Since he was little, he had been taught that Coyote was the cause of much mischief for people and animals, alike.

"What do you want?" Sapariche called down.

They went on staring.

"Go away!" Sapariche said, and resumed his climb.

At the top he looked down again and was surprised to see that the coyotes were halfway up the slope. They had stopped when he did.

"Surely not," Sapariche said. Casting about, he spied a suitable rock. When he was a boy he could hit a tree ten times out of ten but he wasn't a boy any longer and when he threw it, the rock fell well short.

The coyotes stared at the rock and then stared up at him.

Sapariche grunted and hiked on. He had no time to spare for stupid coyotes. He wasn't worried they would try to harm him. Coyotes hardly ever attacked people. It was said they would go after babies and small children and an uncle claimed he knew of a time when a coyote went after a grown woman.

Let them follow. They were probably curious.

Fortunately the going became easier.

The grizzly's tracks were following the tracks of the wagons and the whites had stuck to level stretches as much as possible.

Rather than go over a hill or ridge, they always went around.

Sapariche walked until his legs were bothering him unbearably and his side felt as if a beaver were gnawing at him from the inside out. He halted and frowned at how unfair it was that old age weakened a man when he needed his strength the most.

He took several slow, deep breaths, touched a hand to a braid, and turned to see if the coyotes were still following him.

They were.

Only now they were much closer. They were sitting and watching him.

"You are the strangest coyotes I have ever seen," Sapariche said.

They stared.

Sapariche considered throwing another rock but decided not to. Two coyotes might be more than he could defend against.

He scowled. Talk about bad omens. First the white settlers. Then the grizzly and the loss of his brother and nephew. Then the horse and the wolves. Now this. He wondered if someone had put a curse on him. A skinwalker, perhaps. Or had he offended a witch and not known it?

Or was this a good omen? Were the coyotes there to watch over him?

That was the trouble with omens. Sometimes you never knew if they were good or bad until it was too late.

Squaring his shoulders, Sapariche continued west. He tried not to think about the coyotes. Tried not to imagine that they were creeping closer. They could be on him in a rush before he could unsheath his knife to fight them.

Then and there he decided that if he made it back to his village, he was never leaving it again. He would stay in his lodge where it was comfortable and safe and his knees didn't hurt and his woman would sometimes rub his neck at night.

Suddenly he thought he heard the pad of stealthy paws. He stiffened but kept walking. Above all he must not show fear. Fear drew predators like fresh blood.

STALKED

Some claimed it had a scent all its own and that animals could smell it from far away.

He must not let the coyotes smell his.

He went around a hill, sticking to the middle of the wagon ruts, his hand on his knife. He was tired of worrying. He would confront the pair and see what happened.

With a sharp cry Sapariche turned.

The coyotes were gone.

Sapariche scanned the hill and the forest. He was truly alone. He waited, thinking they might reappear, but no.

Finally he moved on.

"So it was the Trickster, after all," Sapariche said, and laughed. He would have a fine story to tell his wife the next time she rubbed his neck.

All he had to do was live long enough.

Chapter 14

The heavy peal of axes biting into wood rang loud in the valley.

For two days Nate King had been helping Charles, Otto, Hermann and Jacob fell trees for their cabins. None of them, he noted, were in the best physical condition. They couldn't keep at it for very long before needing to rest.

Charles marveled at Nate's stamina. "I don't know how you do it," he remarked while moping his brow with his sleeve on the afternoon of the second day. "And you're older than me."

"Mountain living," Nate said simply. Life in the wilds wasn't for the lazy or the weak. They either stopped being lazy and became strong or they didn't last.

Over at the wagons, Elizabeth and Alice were preparing stew for supper. Freida was mending a shirt.

Bright Rainbow, Clara and Gunther were fetching water from the stream.

"I can't thank you enough for leading us here," Charles said. "This spot is as perfect as can be."

"Just don't let your guard down," Nate cautioned. "I would hate for anything to happen to your families."

"We're safe enough," Charles said blithely. "We'll have the cabins up well before the cold weather hits and have plenty of time to stock up on jerked venison and whatnot."

Nate swung his axe, the blade biting deep. "The trading post at Bent's Fort always has flour and the like on hand. They also carry canned goods."

"We'll pay it a visit the first chance we can," Charles said.

"I could pick things up for you," Nate offered. "Swing by here on our way home."

Charles beamed. "You would do that for us? That would be a great help." He rested the head of his axe on the ground and leaned on the long handle. "I've got to tell you, you're not at all what I expected."

"How so?"

"You're a Mountain Man. The stories we've heard, you're kind are rough and tumble. You swill liquor like water and don't want anything to do with the rest of the human race."

"Tall tales," Nate said.

"You're just like ordinary folks," Charles said. "As nice as can be."

"Until it's time to not be nice," Nate said.

Charles must have thought that was humorous because he chuckled.

"I'm serious. Being neighborly is well and good. But there come times when your life and the lives of those you love are in danger. That's when you have to be not nice."

"Never heard it put that way before," Charles said. "Don't worry. I'm not about to let my wife and children be harmed. I'll do whatever needs doing to protect them."

"The best thing you can do, the smartest thing," Nate said, "is when that time comes, don't hesitate. Don't try to talk yourself out of it. Or feel guilty. Get right to doing."

"I suppose I shouldn't ask," Charles said. "Have you had to kill many men out here? Not just hostiles, I mean."

"You're right," Nate said. "You shouldn't ask." He turned back to the felled tree and swung his axe in a powerful arc.

Charles took that as a hint and didn't ask any more questions.

Nate became absorbed in his work. He settled into a rhythm, sweat beading his brow. He lost all track of time until Winona hollered for him to come eat.

A golden sliver was all that remained of the sun. Soon it would set and evening would fall.

Shouldering the axe, Nate headed for the covered wagons. The others were already there.

Charles and Otto looked weary from their long day of labor. Hermann and Jacob, with the vitality of youth, were joshing with Alice and Bright Rainbow and the smaller children.

Winona presented him with a bowl of soup and a wooden spoon. "Mrs. Walberg made this. You worked so hard, I thought I would bring it to you."

"Thank you," Nate said. "You'll make some man a fine wife one day."

Winona arched an eyebrow. "I thought I have."

Nate dipped his spoon in the soup. "I was thinking we should head out in the morning."

"I was thinking the same thing," Winona said.

"Bright Rainbow will be disappointed but we can't stay forever."

"If you agree, we'll swing by on the way back to check on them," Nate said.

"How wise you are." Winona smirked. "You will make some woman a fine husband one day."

The soup was a little too salty for Nate's taste but he was too hungry to be bothered about it. "You ever have any regrets?"

"About what?"

"Marrying me."

Winona showed her surprise. "Where in the world did that come from? You are as good a husband as any woman could ask for."

"Seeing them," Nate said, nodding at the settlers, "reminds me of when we started out together." He blew on the soup to cool it. "We've been through a lot, you and me."

"And we have a lot more living to do yet," Winona said.

"I hope so. I like being a grandfather," Nate said. He winked at her. "And for a grandmother, you sure can excite a fella."

"Husband!" Winona exclaimed, and blushed. "Keep your voice down. The others might hear."

"I don't care."

"I do."

Affectionate moments like this, Nate truly believed that taking her for his wife was the best thing he ever did.

"We should keep our eyes skinned for that bear on our way down," Winona said. "The little one, Clara, is still worried about it."

"Grizzlies can be scary," Nate said.

"Who would know better than Grizzly Killer?" Winona said.

"You know," Nate said. "That day the Cheyenne warrior saw me kill my first griz?"

"Yes?"

"Good thing it wasn't a frog."

Winona laughed merrily.

Sapariche's stomach was a ravenous wolf that constantly reminded him how hungry it was by rumbling and growling.

Each morning Sapariche was up with the rising of the sun. He nibbled at the deer meat in his pouch and set out. Usually it took considerable walking before his legs stopped aching and his body moved as it should.

He drank water where he found it. Unfortunately, there wasn't much to be found.

He should search for a stream. But he couldn't stop thinking about the grizzly and the settlers. Especially the little white girl. She had gazed on him with such wide, amazed eyes, as if he were the first of his kind she ever saw. He imagined her innocent face reduced to ruin as his nephew's had been, and forged on.

He did not know which was worse. His hunger or his thirst.

Twice he saw squirrels but without a bow there was no way to bring them down. Several times he spied deer but, again, with only a knife, all he could do was daydream of sinking his teeth into their flesh.

That night was the worst yet. He slept fitfully,

tossing and turning and waking up now and again in a cold sweat.

Morning broke chill and cloudy.

Sapariche struggled to get up. He was weak all over and his thoughts were sluggish. He made it to his knees but was unable to stand until he pressed both hands flat on the ground, and pushed. Swaying, he staggered into motion.

The ruts to either side were like old friends. They helped guide him, helped keep him in pursuit of that which no sane person would pursue.

He tried to swallow but his mouth was too dry. Fumbling at his pouch, he found his last piece of venison. Barely the size of his thumbnail, it did little to restore his flagging vitality.

Sapariche wondered if he would die. No one would know what became of him. His people might send warriors to search but even if they found his remains they would not be able to explain how or why he came to his end.

His feet were heavy stones, weighing his legs down.

The sun was well up but for some reason it wasn't giving off much heat. At least, he still felt cold, and would break out in a shiver.

The evil bear was to blame.

A curse on all evil.

Sapariche smiled at how foolish he was being. He tried to concentrate, to marshal his waning strength.

That was when something yipped.

At first Sapariche thought it was a trick of his ears. He was so starved, he was hearing things. But no. The yip was repeated. Strangely enough, it sounded like the sound a fox would make. But why would a fox be yipping at him?

He raised his head and received a shock.

There *was* a fox. A red one. It stood directly in his way with its legs planted, and yipped.

Sapariche shook his head in wonderment. First the wolves, then the coyotes, now a fox. What was going on? They must be omens. If so, their purpose eluded him.

Then he saw something even stranger.

The ground was green and brown with shades in-between. Yet where the fox stood, and in a wide half-circle around it, the ground was red. As bright red as blood.

Sapariche grunted in recognition.

Not *as* blood. Blood. And more. Pieces of hair and bones and hooves crushed by iron teeth and a large head that had been ripped from its body and caved in by a mighty paw.

The head of a cow elk.

"The grizzly!" Sapariche blurted. The beast killed everything the same way it had killed the horse and his brother and nephew. By tearing its prey to bits.

The blood was long dry. Were Sapariche to guess, he would say the elk was slain the day before, perhaps toward evening when elk came out to graze.

The fox had been licking at the blood and the flesh and didn't want to leave.

Drawing his knife, Sapariche slowly advanced. He was in no shape to fight anything and counted on the fox doing as foxes always did when confronted by people.

STALKED

The fox yipped a last time and ran off.

Elated, Sapariche tottered to the grisly remains and fell to his hands and knee. He pried at a piece of flesh, not caring that it had lain there overnight, not caring if it was discolored, not caring about anything except here was food. He placed it in his mouth and winced when his mouth watered so much, it hurt.

He chewed and gulped and picked up another piece. This one had hair on it. He didn't care. He slid it into his mouth, chewed only once, and swallowed.

He was on his fifth piece when a new sound intruded. This time it was a loud stomping noise.

Sapariche sat up as a shadow fell over him.

And everything turned to black.

Chapter 15

Clara was sorry to see the Kings go. She liked Bright Rainbow a lot. Mrs. King too. And she felt safer with Mr. King around. He seemed so sure of himself, unlike her pa, although her pa tried to act as if he were.

It had been two days since the Kings left.

Two days of Clara doing endless chores from after breakfast until dusk. Two days of nothing but work, work and more work.

Her folks told her the family had a lot to do to get ready for winter. Not the least of which was building their cabins and storing food to keep them alive over the colder months.

At one point Jacob mentioned that there would likely be so much snow in the mountains, it might bury their cabin almost to the roof..

Clara figured he was making that up. Her pa had said that he heard the snow sometimes drifted as high as a horse. Her ma heard him and cautioned him to hush and stop scaring Clara but her pa said it was the God's own truth and that he was only letting Clara know what she had to look forward to.

Clara missed South Carolina more each and every day.

The third morning started the same as the others. Up early, a quick breakfast, and they bustled about their tasks.

Clara's first job of the day was to take the bucket to the stream for water. She had done it plenty of times since they arrived.

The sound of axes filled the valley as the menfolk set to preparing logs.

Jacob and Hermann pitched in.

Alice helped the mothers clean up.

Only Gunther had nothing to do and he trailed after Clara.

She was growing used to him hovering. He had gotten over a lot of his shyness but still stammered every now and again.

Watching her dip the bucket in the stream, Gunther said, "Are you still worried about the bear?"

Clara wanted to throw the water on him. "I wish you didn't bring that up. I haven't thought about it all morning."

"My father says we have nothing to be afraid of," Gunther said. "His very words."

Clara didn't see where Mr. Walberg was an authority on bears. From what she'd overheard, he wasn't much of a hunter, either.

"I asked my father if I could carry his pistol," Gunther said. "So I can protect you."

"I don't need protecting," Clara said before she took a moment to think about it.

"He won't let me, anyway," Gunther said. "He thinks I might shoot myself."

"My ma says a pistol won't do much against a bear," Clara remembered.

"We see one, we'll just run," Gunther said.

"Can't do that, either," Clara said, gripping the handle with both hands so she could lift the nearly full bucket out. "Ma says when you run, it provokes them to come after you."

"What do we do then?" Gunther said. "Stand there and let it eat us?"

"Not me. I like being alive." Clara set the bucket on the bank. "Want to give me a hand?"

"Sure."

They each took hold of the handle and between them it was easier.

Clara took a few steps, then abruptly stopped. It forced Gunther to stop short, too, and water sloshed over the sides.

"What's the matter?"

"Listen," Clara said.

Gunther tilted his head. "I don't hear anything."

"That's just it," Clara said. "There's nothing except the axes and our ma's talking."

"So?"

Clara looked behind them. "So a minute ago there were birds singing and a squirrel was raising a ruckus."

"I didn't pay much attention," Gunther said.

Across the stream the wall of vegetation was dark with shadow. Tall trees blocked out much of the sunlight. Within the dark depths, all was still. Not so much as a leaf stirred.

"Do you see something?" Gunther asked.

"No," Clara said. She *felt* something. She felt as if eyes were on them. Her ma might say it was her nerves. She was sure it wasn't.

"Clara?" Gunther said.

She peered deep into the shadows trying to decide if a particularly large one was a thicket or something else.

"Clara?" Gunther said again.

"I'm all right. Let's go." Clara firmed her hold on the handle and they crossed toward the wagons.

"Can I tell you something?" Gunther said.

"Anything," Clara said.

"Promise not to say a word to my parents?"

"Cross my heart and hope to die."

Gunther glanced back at the forest and lowered his voice. "I really don't like it here much."

"Me either," Clara confessed.

"What can we do about it?" Gunther said.

"I guess we have to do like my ma says she does when she has to do something she doesn't like."

"What's that?"

"Grin and bear it."

Sapariche floated in and out of awareness. He would be adrift in a black emptiness and then a faint light would appear and he would hear voices as if they were very far away. Several times he struggled toward them only to sink into the black pit again.

Then, suddenly, he was fully awake.

Stars twinkled high above. He was covered with sweat. He tried to move but was too weak. He was also ice cold. He tried to swallow but his mouth had no spit. He gazed at the stars, wondering if he was dying, and drifted into the abyss yet again.

The next time he opened his eyes it was daylight. The brightness hurt. He squinted and heard low voices and tried to turn his head to see who was talking. He got his head halfway around and then the dark returned.

The next he knew, he was awake once more. The sun was in the sky but not as bright. He wasn't covered with sweat. He lay on his back. Someone had folded his arms on his chest. He felt warmth to one side and heard the crackle of a campfire. His lips were dry and he licked them and turned his head.

Grizzly Killer and his Shoshone woman were seated across the fire, Grizzly Killer sipping from a tin cup, the woman gazing into the distance. Their daughter was chopping roots.

"Friends," Sapariche said barely above a whisper.

The woman came right over. She said something in Shoshone.

"I do not understand," Sapariche said.

"Question," she signed. "How do you feel?"

Sapariche was barely able to move his hands, he was so weak. "I live again," he signed.

Grizzly Killer squatted and signed, "You were very sick. You had a fever. We thought you might die."

Sapariche grunted. He had thought he might die, too.

"Where is your brother?" Grizzly Killer asked.

"Dead," Sapariche signed, and deep sadness flooded through him.

"Your nephew?"

"Dead as well."

The woman whose name Sapariche couldn't remember said something to Grizzly Killer, who fell quiet as she busied herself filling another tin up with water and bringing it to Sapariche so he could drink. Gently, she slid a hand under his head and raised it high enough for her to put the cup to his lips.

It was the most delicious water Sapariche ever tasted. She only let him drink a little and took the cup away. He looked at her in mute appeal.

She said something to Grizzly Killer, who translated in sign.

"If you drink too much you will be sick."

The woman carefully lowered Sapariche's head and spoke some more.

"She will make broth," Grizzly Killer signed. "You must start slow and build your strength."

"I could eat an elk." Sapariche wanted to say more but weariness overcame him and he went under again.

When next he opened his eyes the stars were out and the fire was larger than before.

The woman and the girl were asleep.

Grizzly Killer noticed that he was wake and came closer. "Welcome back," he said in the Ute tongue.

"Thank you for looking after me," Sapariche said.

"You need more," Grizzly Killer said, and resorted to sign. "My wife thinks you came down with food poisoning. You were eating bad meat when we found you."

"I was starving," Sapariche said.

"When a man is hungry enough he will eat anything."

Sapariche grunted in agreement.

"You came a long way on foot," Grizzly Killer said. "Where are your horses?"

"One is dead. The others ran off."

"What happened?"

Only then did Sapariche realize that Grizzly Killer did not know about the bear. He was going to tell him but before he could so much as open his mouth, he fell asleep. He tried to fight it but couldn't.

When he came around the stars still gleamed. The fire was lower.

Grizzly Killer hadn't moved except that his head had dropped to his chest and he was sleeping while sitting up.

"Grizzly Killer?" Sapariche said. His throat was dry and he croaked the words.

Instantly Grizzly Killer was awake. He smiled and said, "Want to eat?"

As much as Sapariche did, he said, "I have something I must say."

"It can wait," Grizzly Killer said. "First you need food." He turned and raised a tin cup that had been placed on a flat rock near the fire. "This is broth," he said. "Do you think you can sit up?"

'No," Sapariche admitted.

Grizzly Killer did as Winona had done and lifted Sapariche's head.

"Slowly," Grizzly Killer cautioned.

It was as delicious as the water. Sapariche savored the warmth that spread down his throat into his chest and belly. He savored, too, that some of his strength returned. Grizzly Killer let him drink the entire cup, and when he lay back down, he felt as if he had gorged himself on a huge meal.

"Are you all right?" Grizzly Killer said.

Sapariche grinned.

"You can have more broth later," Grizzly Killer signed. "Winona says you should have liquids for now. Solid food must wait."

"She is a healer, your woman?"

"She knows a lot about medicines," Grizzly Killer said, his pride in her obvious. "Plants that ease pain and cure."

"My mother was the same," Sapariche said. "My grandmother even more so. People came to her from far off to be healed."

"We will get you back on your feet," Grizzly Killer promised. "Winona says it might be six or seven sleeps before you are able to get around."

Sapariche had a terrible thought. "How long was I unconscious?"

"Three sleeps. This night would have been the fourth."

Sapariche groaned.

"What is wrong?" Grizzly Killer said. "Are you feeling sick?"

"No, no," Sapariche said. "Listen closely. I might fall asleep again and I must say a lot quickly." He took a deep breath. "There is a bear...."

Chapter 16

Clara had never worked so hard in her life.

Back in South Carolina she always had chores. Each day they were pretty much the same. Tote water from the pump first thing every morning. Collect the chicken eggs. Help her ma in the kitchen. Help sweep and clean. Help do laundry.

There was a lot to do but she always had time for herself, too. Hours here and there where she was allowed to play and scamper about and do whatever she pleased.

Since arriving at their new homesite, she didn't have a spare minute to herself.

It was all work, work, and more work.

To be fair, everyone else kept their nose to the grindstone, too.

When Alice grumbled that she was being worked to death, her ma took her to task.

"Quit your griping, girl. Would you rather starve come winter? Or freeze to death? We have to do this. So more backbone and less complaining, if you don't mind, and even if you do."

Clara made sure to hold her own tongue. But she was terribly tired all the time, and at night she fell asleep the instant she laid her head down.

Five days after the Kings left, along about noon,

Hermann took his rifle and went off to find meat for their supper pot. Jacob wanted to tag along but her pa said he was needed to help with the logs.

"Be careful, son," Otto Walberg cautioned his oldest. "Don't wander too far off."

"I won't, father," Hermann dutifully replied.

"Stay alert for Indians," Freida said. "Mr. King said some might happen by now and then."

"I will, mother."

Hermann shouldered his rifle and made for the stream.

Clara watched him cross and enter the forest. Then she devoted herself to helping her ma wash clothes and hang them on a rope strung between the wagons. When that was done they carried the heavy basin a short way and emptied it.

"I want you to know," her ma said as they turned to go back. "Your pa and me are awful proud of how helpful you've been. You don't put on airs like your sister. Sometimes I think that girl believes doing work is too good for her."

"We're all working hard," Clara said.

Her ma placed a hand on her shoulder. "It'll be worth it, little one. Trust me. Once our cabin is built and we're settled in, you'll like it here as much as you ever did back to home."

Clara very much doubted that.

For the next several hours she was kept busy darning holes in her pa's and Jacob's socks. Her mother had taught her how to do it. She liked using the needle. She especially liked the darning eggs. They were made of wood and shaped like real eggs and smooth to the touch. When no one was looking she liked to run her hands over them and sometimes she would juggle them.

By the time she finished the afternoon shadows were lengthening. Because of the towering peaks to the west, the sun disappeared earlier than it would out on the open prairie.

Her ma called her and she went over to where her mother and Mrs. Walberg and Gunther were standing near the supper pot.

"We'd like Gunther and you to take the bucket to the stream and begin filling the pot," her ma said. "It will take three to four trips."

"Women's work," Gunther said.

Mrs. Walberg shook a finger at him. "Men tote water too. And since you're too young to swing an axe, you'll help us and be happy about it."

"Yes, mother," Gunther said, not sounding happy at all.

Clara and him each took hold of the handle and lifted and headed for the stream. "This isn't so bad," she said.

"We haven't gotten to talk much today," Gunther said.

"We will talk all we want once our cabins are built," Clara said. "Everything will be fine then."

"So they keep saying."

"You sound like my sister," Clara teased, and laughed.

Gunther glanced about them, then bent toward her. "You know about Hermann and her, yes?"

"How do you mean? I've seen them together a lot," Clara said.

"They sneak behind the wagons sometimes when they think no one is looking."

"What do they do?"

Gunther twisted his face in disgust. "You know," he said.

"How would I? This is the first I've heard of it."

Gunther lowered his voice even more. "They kiss," he said.

"No!" Clara exclaimed.

"I saw them with my own eyes," Gunther said. "My brother is smitten with her, I think is the word."

"Goodness," Clara said. "If my ma and pa find out, she'll be in trouble."

"My mother knows," Gunther said.

"What did she do?"

"Nothing."

Clara stopped in midstep. "She didn't throw a fit? She's not mad?"

"She didn't act mad when I saw her watching them," Gunther said. "All she did was smile sort of funny and walk away."

"Strange," Clara said. "Our folks punish us when we do wrong."

"Maybe my mother doesn't think it is."

"What can be right about kissing?"

Gunther had no answer to that.

They reached the stream at a point where a gravel strip let them walk right up to the water's edge and drop to their knees to dip the bucket in.

Gunther did the honors, saying, "This water is much colder than our water back home. My father says it is because it comes down from off the mountains."

Clara gazed at the stark peaks. She never imagined mountains could be so high.

"Do you hear that?" Gunther suddenly asked.

"What?" Clara said, and then she did, too. Crackling and rustling in the brush on the other side of the stream.

Something was coming toward them.

Nate King didn't like the idea. He didn't like it one bit. "No," he said bluntly at his wife's proposal.

"Give me a reason?" Winona said.

They were seated only a few feet from Sapariche, who had fallen asleep.

Bright Rainbow was listening with keen interest.

"I can give you lots of them," Nate said. "Hostiles, for starters."

"We're not in hostile territory," Winona pointed out. "The Utes have been friendly to us and few other tribes venture here."

"It's too dangerous," Nate said.

"Since when has that ever stopped us from doing what needs to be done? If we were worried about the dangers we wouldn't live in the mountains."

"I know but...."

"I wasn't done, husband," Winona cut him off, which was rare for her to do. "Our new friends need to be warned. If Sapariche is right and the grizzly is stalking them, they are in great peril. You have tangled with enough grizzlies to know that better than anyone."

"I know but....," Nate tried again.

Winona held up a hand. "One of us must warn them. Ride our horse to the point of exhaustion if need be, but warn them." She paused. "I would go but Sapariche is still sick and weak and I am the better healer." Again Nate went to speak and again she held up her hand. "As it is, it will take you two days to reach the valley. Possibly three."

Nate frowned.

"Besides which," Winona pressed on. "*You* are Grizzly Killer. *You* have killed more of them than any man alive, white or red. I know you did not set out to do that. It sort of happened."

Nate's frown deepened.

"You killed Scar, perhaps the most fearsome grizzly anyone ever heard of."

Nate didn't say anything."

No one, absolutely no one, has as much experience at tracking and slaying grizzlies."

Nate sighed.

"Well?" Winona said.

"You're right. It has to be me."

"Why keep arguing then?"

"I don't want to leave you alone."

"I'm not alone," Winona said. "Bright Rainbow and Sapariche are with me. And need I remind you I am a good shot? And have held my own against Bloods and Apaches and even a wolverine?"

"You're one tough lady," Nate conceded.

"Then we will hear no more of not going," Winona said. ""I will heat you leftover soup and you can be on your way with a full belly and not have to stop until you reach them."

Bright Rainbow cleared her throat and addressed them in Shoshone.

"I would go with my new father."

"Your place is with your mother," Nate said.

"Why do you want to?" Winona asked.

Bright Rainbow gestured. "Clara and Gunther are my friends. They treated me nice."

"You stay with your mother," Nate said.

"I would like to help them," Bright Rainbow insisted, and looked at Winona.

"I understand," Winona said.

Nate inwardly cringed, fearing she was about to give in.

"But your father is right," Winona continued. "He will need to push hard. Harder than you can imagine. If you go, you might slow him up, and above all, he must reach the valley as swiftly as he can."

"You make sense, mother," Bright Rainbow said reluctantly.

"Of course she does," Nate was quick to agree. "Besides, you don't have a lot of experience riding yet." A minor point but valid.

Winona looked at him. "What do you make of the bear?"

"How so?" Nate said.

"Did we not hear the same words from Sapariche? Have you ever heard of a grizzly that tears its victims apart?"

"There's usually not much left when a griz gets done," Nate said.

"You know what I mean. Bits and pieces, Sapariche told us. When has a bear ever done that? What does it mean that this bear does?"

"Hate maybe," Nate speculated. "Could be it was

shot once and holds a grudge."

"Sapariche said it rips everything to pieces, not just people. Horses. Elk. You name it. Does this bear hate all that lives?"

"The important thing is that just like every other bear, it can die."

"So can you, husband."

"That was harsh," Nate said. "I'll make it back to you. Don't you fret."

Winona reached over and placed her hand on his. "You better. I don't want you torn apart."

"Makes two of us," Nate said.

Chapter 17

"*Was ist das?*" Gunther exclaimed.

"What?" Clara said. She was listening to the sounds.

"What is that? A deer?"

Clara didn't think so. Deer were usually quieter. And the sounds seemed to be coming from low down to the ground. Rabbits and squirrels were low to the ground but they never made that much noise.

"Let's get back," Gunther said uneasily.

Clara nodded. "Lift," she said. Together they raised the full bucket and hurried toward the covered wagons. She glanced over her shoulder and saw a thicket near the stream begin to shake.

Another moment and the shaking and the sounds, ceased.

Gunther was walking as fast as he could and pulling on the handle to hurry her along. "Is it coming after us?"

"I don't see anything," Clara said.

"Maybe it was one of those lions," Gunther said.

"A cougar?" Clara shook her head. "Cougars are cats. They're as quiet as anything. They can sneak right up on you and you wouldn't know it."

"Lions. Bears. Wolves. Who knows what else is out there?" Gunther said. "My father and mother should never have brought us here."

"They wanted a new life," Clara said. Just like her own pa.

"They wanted," Gunther said. "Not me."

"Same here," Clara admitted.

Their mothers were still by the supper pot, chatting. Clara's ma took the bucket and upended it and gave it back.

"Fetch more."

"Water?" Clara said.

Her ma laughed. "What else would we put in the stew? Dirt?"

"We heard something," Gunther said.

"An animal?" Mrs. Walberg said.

"I do not know what it was, mother," Gunther said.

"What did it sound like?"

"Branches breaking," Gunther said.

"In the brush," Clara clarified.

"It scared you, did it?" her ma said, grinning.

"No," Clara lied. Upset with herself, she snatched hold of the handle and turned. "Come on, Gunther. Let's get it done."

Falling into step beside her, Gunther said, "You are braver than me."

"I just don't want to be poked fun at," Clara said. "Have them say we're too jittery for our own good because we're kids and all."

"My brother teases me a lot about that."

"My sister teases me," Clara said. "Jacob not so much."

They neared the stream and slowed.

Clara cocked her head. All she heard was the

gurgling of the stream and the chop-chop of axes from beyond the wagons. "Whatever it was, it's probably gone."

"You hope," Gunther said

They went on. The forest stayed still except for the warbling of a robin.

"See?" Clara said. "It's safe."

Gunther let her lead him to the water's edge and helped her dip the bucket. "Let's be quick about it."

"We're fine, I tell you."

"Let me tell *you* something," Gunther said. "I have been having dreams. Terrible dreams. Where I am attacked and my blood is everywhere."

"What attacks you?"

"I never see it. It comes out of the darkness and I scream and run."

"A nightmare. I have them too."

"The same one three times?"

"That happens sometimes," Clara said. She pushed harder on the bucket so it lowered and would fill faster. Glancing at the thicket, she was relieved to see a butterfly flitting about. It must mean everything was all right.

She smiled, watching the butterfly, trying to remember if she ever saw one like it back in South Carolina. It dipped and rose and flew to the right and then to the left and dipped again until it was only a few inches above the ground. Wings slowing, it alighted.

"What do you see?" Gunther asked anxiously.

"Nothing," Clara said. She was growing annoyed with him.

The butterfly was still on the ground.

No, Clara realized. Not on the ground itself but on something *on* the ground. Something pale. No rock was that color. A clump of dead grass? she asked herself. But no. Dead grass was usually a tan sort of color. Puzzled, she rose for a better view.

The pale thing looked to be partially curled, with something sticking out it. In fact, several somethings.

Clara had never seen the like.

"The bucket is full," Gunther let her know.

Grunting, Clara helped lift it and started to turn to go back but stopped. "Hold up."

"What for?"

"Set it down," Clara said, and lowered her side before he could object. He quickly followed suit to keep from spilling it.

"What's going on?"

Clara pointed at the strange shape at the base of the thicket. "Do you see that?"

Gunther came around to her side. "See what? The trees? The brambles?"

"No, silly," Clara said. "Do you see what the butterfly is standing on?"

"Butterfly?" Gunther shielded his eyes from the glare of the sun. "That little green one? What about it?"

"What's under it?"

"Grass. A rock. Who can say?"

"Look closer."

Gunther looked at her, instead. "What does it matter? Let us take the water back."

Clara wanted to cross and see but she was loathe to get her shoes wet. Her mother would be upset. She rose onto her toes but it didn't help.

"I really want to go," Gunther said. "Please, Clara. This is silly."

Clara thought he was a fine one to talk but she sighed and helped him lift the bucket and started off. "Aren't you ever curious about anything?"

"Not butterflies."

Clara sighed a second time. She had hoped that Gunther would make a fine friend to play with but he was too serious about everything. "Consarn it, I need to know." So saying, she abruptly lowered her side of the bucket and water spilled onto Gunther's leg.

"Hey!"

"I'm going to take a look. You can come or not." Turning, Clara marched to the stream. The butterfly was still there, lazily moving its wings, evidently enjoying the sun and the warmth.

Although her ma would be mad at her, Clara picked the shallowest point and waded across, walking on her toes so as not to soak her shoes.

Light splashing told her that Gunther had tagged along.

She came to the other side and smiled as he joined her. "See? We're still alive!"

Gunther gazed apprehensively at the forest. "Are you always going to be this way?"

"What way?" Clara faced the thicket.

The butterfly was sitting still.

She took a slow step, not wanting to spook it. The shape of the thing it was perched on finally became clear.

"Why, that's a hand!" Gunther blurted.

A cold sensation swept from Clara's chest clear down to her feet. The hand was attached to an arm in a brown shirt. Both were spattered with red drops.

Blood.

Fresh blood.

To her amazement, the butterfly had its head bent over one of the drops and its probiscis, she remembered her ma calling that part, was moving up and down as if the butterfly were drinking from the drop.

Gunther gasped. "*Gott*! I know that shirt! It's Hermann's!"

They glanced at once another and Gunther went to flee but Clara grabbed his arm.

"We have to see!"

"Let go!" Gunther said, tying to pull loose.

"He's your brother!" Clara said.

Gunther swallowed, and nodded.

Clara inched forward. From this new angle she could see the entire arm and part of a shoulder but the rest of Hermann was hidden by the thicket. All that crackling they heard earlier, she realized, was him crawling toward their camp. He had gotten this far and collapsed.

"We should yell for our parents," Gunther whispered.

"Not yet."

"Why not?"

"We need to see if he's alive," Clara said. She was sure that was what her folks would do. She tentatively reached out and parted the thicket enough to see Hermann's head and chest. He lay face-down.

"Hermann?" Gunther whispered. "Brother, can you

hear me?"

Hermann didn't move.

There wasn't any blood in his hair or on his back. It made Clara wonder where the blood came from. She placed her hand on Hermann's and shook it. "Hermann? It's us! Your brother and Clara."

"I am going for my father!" Gunther said.

"Hermann?" Clara said. She parted the thicket more. Now she could see Hermann's belt and his backside but not his legs. They were in high grass.

"Will you *please* listen to me!" Gunther pleaded.

Clara squeezed in closer. Thin branches poked her and she was scratched on the wrist. "Help me drag him into the open."

"He is too big," Gunther said. "Too heavy."

"Together we can do it," Clara said. She took hold of the remaining arm.

"You don't care how I feel," Gunther protested, but he bent and gripped the belt.

"On three," Clara said, and counted, "One. Two. Three."

They pulled for all they were worth, straining until Gunther was red in the face and Clara's own felt hot. All they succeeded in doing was moving Hermann a few inches. He was too big, his body too wide, for them to force it through the thicket.

"*Now* can I go fetch my father?" Gunther pleaded.

"Maybe if I push and you pull," Clara said. Turning sideways, she sought to squeeze farther in. The branches impeded her.

"My father will be furious when he hears we did not run to him right away," Gunther said.

"Don't tell him."

"That wouldn't be right."

Clara was able to go as far as Hermann's belt. She had averted her face to keep her eyes from being poked. Now she carefully pushed a few more branches aside so she could turn her head.

"Hermann? Hermann?" Gunther tugged at his brother's arm. "Is he even breathing? Can you tell."

"No," Clara said, although his chest didn't appear to be rising and falling. She looked to see if Hermann's legs were straight behind him or bent to either side.

For a few seconds she was riveted in shock.

Then she opened her mouth to scream.

Chapter 18

Hermann Walberg's legs weren't lying straight or bent.

They weren't there.

From the bottom of his backside to where his feet should be, there was nothing but blood soaked grass. His legs had been ripped off. Strips of ragged flesh dangled below what was left.

Clara's scream froze in her throat.

That was because of a loud crunch that drew her terrified gaze to the reason Hermann's legs were no longer attached to his body.

Beyond the thicket was a small clearing. One of Hermann's legs lay in the grass, the knee bent, the foot bizarrely raised toward the sky.

The other leg was in the mouth of the monster responsible.

A huge grizzly.

'The' grizzly, Clara was sure. The same one she saw before. As she looked on, it bit down with another loud crunch.

Pure and utter terror gripped her.

Gunther mewed like a kitten.

The grizzly ignored them. It went on chewing at the leg much as a dog might chew at a bone.

Clara gulped. Whirling, she snatched Gunther's

wrist and fled. Or tried to.

Gunther staggered, tripped, and would have fallen if she hadn't flung an arm around him to hold him up. "My brother!" he bleated.

The grizzly stopped chewing and turned its head toward them.

"Run!" Clara wailed. She pulled fit to yank Gunther's arm off. He stumbled, recovered, and raced at her side. She came to the stream and plowed through the water, not caring how wet she got her shoes. Her ma's anger was the least of her worries. On reaching the other side she dashed past the bucket and glanced back.

The grizzly wasn't after them.

"Faster!" Clara bawled, and flew as fast as her legs would move.

Over at the wagons, both their mothers and Alice looked around.

To Clara's surprise it was her sister who reacted first and ran to meet them.

Clara had tears in her eyes and her breaths came in great gasps.

Gunther was crying and saying, "No! No! No!"

Clara glanced back again, and tripped. She sprawled flat and was about to scramble up when her sister was there, holding her.

"What's wrong? What's the matter?"

Tears flowing, Clara tried to answer but couldn't. Her ma got there. So did Mrs. Walberg.

Gunther flung himself against her legs and clung hold.

"What in the world?" Clara's ma said, and looked toward the forest. "What is it, child?"

In a rush Clara got it out. "Hermann's dead! His legs ripped off! The bear, ma! It's that awful bear!"

"My Hermann dead?" Mrs. Walberg said, and rocked back on her heels. Scooping Gunther up, she started toward the stream.

"Freida, no!" Clara's ma yelled, and grabbed hold of Mrs. Walberg.

"Let go!" Freida said, trying to tear free.

"Think, Freida! In God's name, think! The bear will kill you and Gunther, too!"

Mrs. Walberg had tears in her eyes. She shook her head, and began doing as Gunther had done, saying over and over, "No! No! No!"

Clara's ma said, "Alice! Fetch the men and Jacob! Go! Now! This instant!"

For once Alice did exactly as their ma wanted and was off like a bolt.

"To the wagons!" her ma cried. "We need to get to the wagons!"

Clara wanted to get as far as possible from the grizzly. She let her mother pull her and looked back. The thicket was shaking. For a few heart-rending moments she thought the grizzly was about to burst out after them, but no. The shaking stopped and the grizzly didn't appear.

Mrs. Walberg gave voice to several loud sobs. Gunther was still crying.

Clara was glad when they came to the wagons and her ma let go and she could sink to her knees. She felt weak, confused, terrified.

Her ma darted to their wagon, climbed in, and reappeared with one of their pistols.

Clara doubted it would do much good. As big as the bear was, shooting it might only make it mad. She remembered he pa telling them about an uncle who shot a black bear but the bear didn't die. Instead, it attacked and hurt her uncle so badly he was laid up for half a year.

Her ma faced the stream and held the pistol in both hands, a thumb curled around the hammer. "I will by heaven shoot it!" she declared.

Clasping Gunther to her bosom, Mrs. Walberg sagged against her wagon. More tears flowed and she gasped, "My Hermann! My wonderful Hermann!"

In her mind Clara saw the legless body and the leg sticking out both sides of the bear's mouth. A mouth that big, the grizzly could probably bite her in half.

"What's keeping the men?" her ma said.

A new fear jolted Clara. What if the bear had killed them? Or what if it attacked Alice before she could reach them. Oh, Lord, Lord, Lord. She wanted to curl into a ball and shut the world out and pray it was all a nightmare.

"We never should have come here!" Mrs. Walberg said. "We should have gone on to Oregon Country!"

"How were we to know?" Clara"s ma said.

"Otto shouldn't have listened to your husband!" Mrs. Walberg said. "He should have done as I wanted and gone to Oregon!"

"You can't blame Charles for this!" her ma said.

Her eyes filled with tears, her cheeks slick, her nose running, Mrs. Walberg said angrily, "I can and I will! I was foolish and let Otto agree even though I knew it was the wrong thing to do!"

"*Now* you bring this up?" her ma said.

"You heard your child!" Mrs. Walberg said. "My Hermann is dead! My first born! You're a mother! You know what that means!"

Clara didn't. Dead was dead. What difference did it make who was born first or second or last?

Mrs. Walberg raised her face to the sky. "May God forgive me for not speaking my peace when I should have! And now my Hermann.....!" She lowered her chin and sobbed.

Clara's own tears were lessening. She was still afraid the bear would attack them but she was also becoming mad. Mad that she had been right about the bear following them and no one believed her. Mad that poor Hermann had been slain. Mad that Mrs. Walberg would dare to blame her pa. And maddest of all at the bear. Why couldn't it leave them alone?

Boots pounded, and her pa and Mr. Walberg and Jacob came running around the front of the other wagon, her pa and Jacob carrying rifles, Mr. Walberg only an axe. Alice was close behind.

Mr. Walberg was as pale as snow. "What is this about Hermann?" he said to his wife. "Tell me it is not so!"

Mrs. Walberg uttered a piercing wail.

"*Gott im Himmel*!" Mr. Walberg exclaimed.

Alice came to Clara and placed her arm around Clara's shoulders. "Are you all right, sis?"

Clara had never seen her sister so concerned. It shocked her.

Her pa was listening to something her ma was saying in his ear. He glanced at Mrs. Walberg and frowned, then hefted his rifle and said to Mr. Walberg, "We must go after it, Otto. Now. While it's close."

"My son," Mr. Walberg said softly

"I know," her pa said. "We must kill the grizzly before it kills any more of us."

Mrs. Walberg, still hugging Gunther, said, "Are you out of your mind? It will do to you as it did to our Hermann!"

"It likely took Hermann by surprise," her pa said. "We'll be ready for it."

"I don't want my Otto to go," Mrs. Walberg said.

"We let that bear get away, it will come back," her pa said. "Mark my words."

"We have already marked too many of them," Mrs. Walberg said.

"What does that mean?"

"My husband listens to you too much."

Mr. Walberg stepped between them. "No, Freida. Charles is right. We must kill the bear while we can. Otherwise we will never be safe for as long as we live here."

"We are not living here. We're leaving," Mrs. Walberg said.

"What?" Clara's pa said.

"I mean it, Otto," Mrs. Walberg said. "We bury Hermann and we set out for Oregon Country as we originally planned."

"I have a say in whether we stay or not," Mr. Walberg said.

An argument was about to break out. Clara silenced them both by yelling, "Listen! All of you! Don't you hear it!"

Her ma gasped, "My word!"

From across the stream, from the other side of the thicket, rose a loud racket. Growls and snarls mixed with grunts and sounds no human throat could make.

At first it sounded to Clara as if the grizzly were fighting something. But no. All the sounds seemed to come from the same bear.

"Charles?" her ma said nervously.

"I never heard the like before," her pa replied. He clasped Mr. Walberg's shoulder. "Are you with me or not, Otto? This might be your best chance to avenge Hermann."

"Just the two of us?" Mr. Walberg said.

"I'm going with you," Jacob said.

"No," her pa said. "You're staying with the ladies and the children."

"I'm hardly a child," Alice said.

Clara still had her ears cocked for sounds from beyond the thicket. They were tapering off. Or perhaps the bear was moving farther away. Before she could stop herself she heard herself say, "I'd like to go too."

"No," both her pa and her ma said at the same time.

"Don't be ridiculous," her ma went on. "You're too young. You don't have a gun and you wouldn't hardly know how to use one if you did. Leave this to the grownups."

"You going is silly," Jacob said.

"You get to," Clara bristled.

"Both of you are staying here," her pa ended their spat. Wedging the stock of his rifle to his shoulder, he looked at Mr. Walberg, who nodded and hurried to his wagon and came back with his own rifle.

"Let us do this."

"Oh, husband," Mrs. Walberg said.

Clara had every intention of staying put. Making her pa angry would be plumb foolish. So when both fathers reached the stream and headed across, she was as surprised as anyone that her body had a mind of its own. Before she could stop herself, she was flying after them.

"Clara Jane!" her ma shouted.

Clara couldn't say what made her do it beyond the fact that she wanted to see the bear die. She needed to see that if she was to ever again enjoy a good night's sleep.

Only when she reached the stream did it strike her how dangerous this was.

First it had been Hermann.

The next to die might be her.

Chapter 19

Nate King pushed his bay as hard as he dared. As much as he wanted to warn the settlers, riding his horse into the ground would defeat his purpose.

He avoided steep slopes as much as possible and stopped whenever the bay showed signs of tiring.

It tore at him to leave Winona. Yes, the settlers were in danger. Yes, he agreed with her that he should try and help them if he could.

Still.

Nate disliked being separated from her. When he was a lot younger he hadn't minded so much. During trapping season he'd often be gone for weeks at a time. But that was then.

The beaver trade had dwindled. Fickle Easterners never stuck with any one fashion for long, and the beaver craze went the way of countless others.

Added incentive for him to stay close to home came with the births of Zach and Evelyn. To have children, to be a family, came to mean everything to him.

That both were now married and lived in cabins of their own filled him with pride. Every parent knew that their offspring eventually left the nest. It was a given that came with maturity. But he had moments where he dearly missed those early days when Zach and Evelyn were little and Winona's and his entire lives revolved around being the best parents they could be.

He supposed he should be thankful that both his son and his daughter chose to live in the same valley he did. That they weren't more than a rifle shot away was a comfort.

Thinking of King Valley made him think of the valley he had led the settlers to, and the danger they were in.

To hear Sapariche tell it, this particular grizzly was the devil incarnate. Sapariche claimed that the bear didn't just kill---it ripped its victims to shreds.

Nate had never heard of such a thing. Even Scar, the legendary griz he hunted down and killed for the Utes, killed in the usual manner.

Except.....

Except Scar had unleashed his wrath on a particular village. Just the one. Again and again, Scar killed members of that particular band and only that band. No one ever knew why.

This new grizzly was no Scar. But it did seem to be driven by a single-minded lust to slay.

A normal bear wouldn't stalk prey over endless miles, either. Over short distances, yes. But not days on end.

If Sapariche was right, this griz was unusual in other ways, too.

Its ferocity, for instance. Hungry grizzlies killed anything they could catch. They did so quickly, and once their prey was down, they fed. They didn't do what this one was doing and rip their prey to bits.

Based on what the bear did to Sapariche's brother and nephew, and the stallion, Nate suspected there was something more to the killings than simple hunger.

It was almost as if this bear killed out of rage.

Or hate.

Or....and Nate's next thought jolted him.

Was it possible the grizzly tore its prey to bits for the sheer savage pleasure of doing so?

Nate had heard of people who murdered others for the thrill of it.

Was this grizzly the same?

Nate gave his head a toss and buckled down to riding. Whether hate, rage or pleasure, the bear must be stopped.

God willing, he would reach the settlers in time.

If not.......

Clara's ma was still shouting her name as Clara splashed across the stream.

Her pa and Mr. Walberg were lost to view. They had gone around the thicket.

Clara ran faster to catch up. Part of her knew she should stop and go back but another part drove her on around to where she drew up short to keep from colliding with Mr. Walberg.

Both he and her pa was staring at bright pools of blood and pieces of flesh and clothing that had once been a leg.

Of Hermann there was no sign. A wide scarlet stain led deeper into the woods.

"The brute has dragged my son off!" Mr. Walberg exclaimed in horror.

Her pa nodded and firmed his hold on his rifle. "Side by side, Otto. You watch left, I'll watch right."

Shoulder to shoulder they cautiously advanced.

Clara was in luck. Neither noticed her. She hung back until they were under the trees then crept forward, careful to avoid stepping in the blood.

A tiny voice in her head screamed at her to stop. She ignored it. Why, she couldn't say. She sensed it was important to see what became of Hermann.

The forest was deathly still. So much so, Clara could hear the thumping of her own heart. She stayed poised on the balls of her feet, ready to run at the first hint of the bear.

Mr. Walberg coughed. "Do not be offended by what my wife said, friend Charles."

"I'm not," her pa said.

"She is upset. Her heart is broken...."

"Otto," her pa interrupted. "Now's not the time."

"Oh. Yes. Sorry."

The blood trail brought them to another clearing. The two fathers entered it and suddenly stopped, Mr. Walberg letting out a gasp.

"God Almighty!" her pa said.

Clara edged to where she could see past them. At first she couldn't make hide nor hair of what she saw other than a lot of blood mixed with pink chunks and other different colors.

Mr. Walberg groaned. "My Hermann! My poor Hermann!"

"He was dead when the bear did this," her pa said.

Did what? Clara asked herself. The answer dawned in a flash of new fear. Those pink parts were flesh. The others were swatches of Hermann's clothes.

"Where is his head?" Mr. Walberg said.

"I don't see it anywhere," her pa told him.

Clara became dizzy. Her own head swam and she swayed and almost fell.

"Clara? What in the world!"

She might have collapsed if not for an arm that was suddenly around her.

It was her pa. "What are you doing here, girl?"

Before Clara could answer, feet pounded and her ma and her sister came running up.

"Clara Gordon! What has gotten into you?" her ma fumed. "Didn't you hear me yelling---." Her ma stopped with her mouth half-open.

Alice thrust a hand over her own mouth as if to keep from screaming.

Clara's pa practically pushed her toward her ma, saying, "Take her, Elizabeth! Go! Now! This is no place for her or for any of you!"

Her ma stepped closer to the gore. "Is that what's left of Hermann?"

"I am afraid so, Mrs. Gordon," Mr. Walberg said, tears trickling down his ruddy cheeks. "A creature that would do this---."

"The bear," Clara said.

Her ma gazed fearfully about and turned and took Clara's hand. "Back to the wagons with you! Alice, you too!"

Her hand still over her mouth, her eyes as wide as saucers, Alice nodded and backed away.

"What will I tell my Freida?" Mr. Walberg said to no one in particular.

Clara's ma stopped and looked at her pa. "All of us should go! This instant!"

"We have to go after the bear," her pa said.

"Like blazes you do!" her ma said angrily. "You're escorting us back."

Her pa hefted his rifle. "We need to kill it! It's close! We can track it easy, I bet, with the trail this fresh."

"Did you ever think," her ma said, "that it wants you to go after it?"

"That's ridiculous," her pa said. He turned to Mr. Walberg. "Tell her, Otto. We have to avenge Hermann while we still have plenty of daylight left."

Mr. Walberg was staring forlornly at the pink pieces and the blood. He didn't say anything. His cheeks were wet from weeping, and a drop fell from the tip of his chin.

"Otto?"

"He's in no shape to avenge anything! Consarn it, Charles!" her ma said. "Think of me and the girls! If anything happens to you, we're left stranded in the middle of nowhere!" Her voice took on a pleading tone. "Please! Come back with us!"

Her pa was staring at Mr. Walberg. "I can't do it alone, Otto."

Mr. Walberg still didn't respond.

"See?" her ma said. "Use common sense. The bear followed us this far, it's not likely to leave us be. It will stick around and come after another of us."

"You don't know that," her pa said. "I never heard of a bear doing such a thing."

Clara was deathly afraid her pa would march off into the woods by his lonesome. He could be stubborn at times. Not that she would say so to his face. But her ma had, more than once.

"Damnation!" her pa said.

"Enough of that kind of talk," her ma said. "Come on! Mr. Walberg, you as well."

Mr. Walberg just stood there.

Her pa went to him and placed a hand on his forearm. "Otto?"

"He was such a good boy," Mr. Walberg said softly.

Her pa gently pulled and Mr. Walberg slowly turned and let himself be led.

"Everyone stay close!" her ma said. "Alice, you too."

The five of them retraced their steps to the stream.

Clara fearfully kept her gaze on the woods behind them. She half expected the grizzly to come charging out. She very much doubted her pa would be able to stop it. Nor could Mr. Walberg, the state he was in.

When they reached the other side, her ma gave her arm a hard shake.

"Don't you ever run off like that again! The next time you do, I'll tan your backside so you won't be able to sit for a week."

"I'm sorry, ma," Clara said, although she really wasn't.

"We are in terrible trouble."

Her pa muttered something, then said, "Don't scare the girl like that. I can protect her. Protect all of you. All I need is one shot."

Clara remembered something. "Mr. King told me grizzlies are hard to die."

"They're flesh and blood," her pa said. "They might be tougher than the black bears we're used to back home but they bleed the same as any animal and if I can put lead into it, this grizzly will fall the same as any other bear."

"You have a plan for killing it without getting killed yourself?" her ma said.

"Not yet," her pa said.

"Didn't think so."

"What's gotten into you, Elizabeth?" her pa said. "You've hardly ever talked to me this way."

"I'm scared, Charles," her ma said. "For all of us."

"I will handle this," her pa said. "Trust me."

Clara would very much like to. Her pa had always been a man of his word. When he said he would do something, he did it. Like the time he shot a fox that was raiding their chicken coop.

Only thing was, a fox wasn't as fearsome as a grizzly.

Not anywhere close.

Chapter 20

That evening the adults made not one, not two, but three fires. They also gathered large piles of wood to last the night through.

There was plenty of space between the fires for everyone to sit or lie down.

Clara's pa and Mr. Walberg had decided that they were going to sleep in the open, protected by the fires. Both were of the opinion that bears, like most animals, were afraid of fire, and theirs would keep the grizzly away.

Besides, no one wanted to be cooped up in a wagon where the bear could sneak up on them without them knowing it was there.

Clara sat hugging her legs to her chest and listening to the hubbub. Gunther sat close by.

As for the rest, her pa and Mr. Walberg were huddled by one fire, her ma and Mrs. Walberg at another. Alice sat by her lonesome and occasionally sniffing. She was taking the death of Hermann hard. Jacob was close to the men, all three of them with rifles in their laps.

Gunther leaned toward Clara. "I want to go home."

"Me too," Clara confessed.

"How can your father want us to stay after what happened?"

"He'd like for this to be our new home. If he kills the bear, it can."

"We will end up like my brother."

Clara was inclined to agree. To her way of thinking, their puny fires wouldn't keep the grizzly away. She'd had a bad feeling about this bear ever since she first saw it.

Just then her ma and Mrs. Walberg rose and went over to the men, who looked up.

"We've been talking it over, Charles," her ma said. "We've decided to leave first thing in the morning."

"You've decided?" her pa said. "Us men don't have a say?"

Her ma jabbed a finger at him. "Don't you dare! This is too serious. Us womenfolk have as much right to our opinions as you men."

"And in our opinion," Mrs. Walberg cut in, "we must leave while the rest of us are still breathing."

Clara's pa glanced toward Clara and Gunther. "Don't talk like that around the children. You'll scare them."

"They're already scared," her ma said. "All of us are."

Mrs. Walberg turned to her husband and jabbed a finger. "Tell him, Otto."

"Freida....," Mr. Walberg sort of mumbled.

"Tell him!" Mrs. Walberg said. "Just because you are fond of the man is no reason to let him browbeat you."

"Browbeat?" her pa said, rising. "I resent that. Your husband and I have talked over every decision we've made and both of us had to agree or we wouldn't do it."

"Otto lets himself be persuaded too easily," Mrs. Walberg said.

"Freida," Mr. Walberg said, but no one paid him any mind.

Clara wished they would stop squabbling. She liked it better when they all got along. She stared off into the darkness and stiffened when part of the dark seemed to move. A very large part of the dark.

"Our Hermann is gone," Mrs. Walberg was saying, "and I will not lose Gunther too. We are leaving, Otto. Tell him we are leaving."

Squinting against the glare of the fire, Clara sought more sign of movement. She saw none and was beginning to relax when a huge rounded shape appeared between the covered wagons and the stream.

Mr. Walberg said, "We were talking about killing the bear. If we do that, we can stay, surely?"

"The two of you against that monster?" Mrs. Walberg said.

"I'll help," Jacob said.

Clara shut them out. The shape had grown. It was coming closer but still wasn't near enough for her to make out what it could be. It might be the grizzly. Or it might be that buffalo.

A finger touched her arm and she nearly jumped.

"What is that?" Gunther whispered.

"Don't know yet," Clara whispered back.

Her ma raised her voice. "The only helping you'll be doing, Jacob, is staying close to camp and help protect your sisters and the rest of us. You're not going off into the woods after that thing, and that's final."

"Ah, ma," Jacob said. "Pa will need me to watch his

back."

"No and no," their ma said.

Clara's breath caught in her throat as part of the shape became distinct enough for her to see the great head and the ears and the long muzzle. And eyes that appeared to gleam in the reflected firelight.

"*Gott!*" Gunther wheezed.

Once again Clara's voice didn't want to work. This time, though, she sucked in a deep breath, leaped to her feet, pointed and screamed, "The bear! The grizzly is here!"

Gunther jumped up, too. "There! There!" he cried.

In a scramble everyone else closed around them with her pa and Mr. Walberg moving to the front with their rifles leveled.

"Where?" Her pa said. "I don't see...."

The grizzly took another step and all of them saw its enormous head and shoulders and its hump, outlined against the backdrop of night. It stood staring at them.

"Shoot!" Alice shouted.

"I don't have a good shot," their pa said. "If I wound it, it will be out for our blood."

"It already is!" Alice said.

"Why isn't it doing anything?" Mrs. Walberg said.

Clara was mesmerized by those awful eyes. They bored into her like knives, a terrible sensation that rendered her weak at the knees. She was vaguely aware that her ma had spun away and now was back, holding a brand from the fire.

"Be gone, you devil!"

Her ma threw the firebrand.

It flew in a blazing arc, letting off sparks of red and

orange, and landed a good three feet from the grizzly.

Clara opened her mouth to scream, sure the bear would attack. Instead, it moved close to the brand, sniffed noisily a few times, then unexpectedly melted into the darkness without so much as a growl.

"Why, I scared it off!" her ma exclaimed, and laughed.

"That bear's not so tough," Jacob said. "Let's go after it, pa. You too, Mr. Walberg."

"My Otto will do no such thing," Mrs. Walberg said. "I won't---." She stopped and said, "Listen!"

Clara heard it, too. Loud splashing from the direction of the stream. Something was running in the water. Something big. The splashing became louder as the thing---it had to be the grizzly---came closer to their wagons.

Suddenly the noise stopped.

"What on earth?" Mrs. Walberg said.

Mr. Walberg was also confused. "What was that about?"

Jacob said, "It came up the stream and now it must be on the other side of your wagon."

"Is it creeping up on us?" Mrs. Walberg said.

"I would hardly call that creeping," Mr. Walberg told her.

"Could be it has gone off into the forest," her pa said.

Suddenly there was a tremendous crash and the Walbergs' wagon shook violently. From under the canvas came the harsh sounds of objects falling and smashing.

Everyone turned to living rock.

STALKED

A second crash, louder and more violent, followed the first. So violent that the wheels on the off side lifted a few inches off the ground and thudded down again.

A roar filled the night.

"We have to stop it!" her pa yelled, and went to run around the wagon.

Her ma grabbed his arm with both hands and brought him to a stop. "No you don't! Run! All of you, run!"

Mrs. Walberg grabbed Gunther's hand in one of hers and pushed her husband with the other, bellowing, "Do as she says! We must get clear! Move, Otto, move!"

Jacob took a step toward the wagon but their ma practically screeched at him.

"Don't you dare! Take your sisters and run!"

Clara didn't know where they could go that the grizzly couldn't get them. She felt her arms seized, Jacob on one side and Alice on the other.

Her pa was still struggling with her ma.

"Let go, Elizabeth!"

"No!" her ma yanked on his arm for all she was worth.

"I may not have another chance like this!"

"Run, damn you, Charles! Your family comes first!"

Clara was shocked at hearing her ma cuss. Were she to say that, she'd have her mouth washed out with soap. "Pa! Please!" she hollered. She was certain that if he went around the wagon, she would never see him again. Or if she did, he would be in bits and chunks.

Her pa reluctantly joined the exodus.

As a third blow shook the wagon, they ran on out

of the circle of firelight to the edge of the darkness. Pressed close together, they listened, helpless, as the grizzly slammed into the Walberg's wagon over and over.

Clara couldn't understand why it was attacking the wagon and not them. She was glad, though.

The wagon tilted with each impact. Came another, and the wheels on the other side left the ground entirely. For a few heartbeats the wagon hung slanted at the stars. Then down it smashed, creating a din of breaking and cracking and ruin.

The bonnet buckled and split and personal effects came tumbling out.

"Our belongings!" Mrs. Walberg wailed.

"We should keep running!" Alice yelled.

"Stay put!" their ma shouted. "We must stick together!"

Clara was too paralyzed to move.

A small bundle of clothes had spilled from the wagon and rolled close to a fire. So close, the bundle gave off smoke and then burst into flame. The flames, in turn, licked at a flap of canvas. Fashioned from cotton duck fabric, it caught quickly. More flames spread, rapidly engulfing half of the bonnet.

Mrs. Walberg uttered a piercing cry and tore at her hair.

"All my things!" Gunther said.

"What if it spreads to our wagon?" Alice said.

"Oh, my Lord!" Mr. Walberg exclaimed. "The whale oil!"

Clara remembered that he had brought some all the way from Pennsylvania. In a jar he never opened. He was saving it for use during the winter months.

"What about it?" her ma said.

Her pa spun. "Dear God! Everyone down! Get on the ground this instant!"

Clara started to obey---and the night exploded.

Chapter 21

There was a loud *crump* and then a blast that rang Clara's ears.

Sheets of flame erupted toward the sky, lighting up the scene as bright as day. In a twinkling the Walberg wagon was engulfed in fire. Flaming pieces of the bonnet rose into the air like so many small glowing birds. Some sputtered and fell in the grass.

Some fell on the other wagon. Wisps of smoke began curling from the duck cloth.

"Lord, no!" her ma cried.

"We've got to save it!" her pa yelled, and started forward, only to draw up short as a huge darkling shape appeared.

"The grizzly!" Alice screamed.

Clara's tongue was rooted to the roof of her mouth. In the light of the fire, the great bear's eyes glowed like red coals.

All it did was stand there, staring.

The next moment her family's wagon burst into flames, the bonnet catching like so much tinder.

Her ma let out a wail.

Her pa cussed like she never heard him cuss before.

Clara felt something brush her arm and then her brother was running toward their wagon, shouting something about putting it out. Her ma screamed at him to stop and her pa took a few quick steps after him.

The grizzly was ungodly quicker, doom given sinew, with a speed that belied its bulk.

Jacob was concentrating on the wagon and didn't notice.

"Jacob!" Clara found her voice.

Her brother glanced toward them and then must have heard the bear or sensed it because he whirled and tried to bring his rifle to his shoulder but compared to the enormous mountain of muscle charging him, he was molasses.

The grizzly didn't leap on him or swing a paw to rip and rend. It yawned its maw wide and without breaking stride clamped its mouth closed on either side of Jacob's head.

Jacob didn't cry out. He didn't shriek or curse. His body jerked once and he went limp and the grizzly wheeled and headed for the the woods.

It happened so fast.

Clara's pa fired and Mr. Walberg fired but apparently their shots had no effect because the grizzly didn't react. It made off carrying Jacob as if her brother were a stick and the griz was a dog.

Her ma screeched fit to rupture her lungs.

"No! No! No!" her pa shouted. He was frantically reloading.

Mr. Walberg was reloading, too, but much slower. "Charles!" he said. "Charles!"

Her pa wasn't listening. He was stumbling toward the wagons and uttered a loud sob. "Not my boy! Not my boy!"

Both wagons were burning, the crackle of the

flames like the crackle of bacon in a frying pan only a thousand times louder.

Clara realized the oxen were bawling and pulling at their tethers. One was already loose. The others had no trouble doing the same and together they lumbered toward the east end of the valley and the way down into the foothills .

There was no sign of their horses.

Her pa dropped to a knee.

Her ma ran to him and gripped him by the shoulders and turned him so he faced her and shook him. She said something and he pa numbly nodded and let her raise him to his feet.

"We need to get out of here!" Alice said. "We need to run!"

Run where? Clara wondered.

Both wagons were roaring infernos giving off thick smoke and a legion of sparks. Glass popped and an acrid smell tingled Clara's nose.

Her ma and pa rejoined them and her ma grabbed her hand and said, "Come on, child!"

No one said anything as they headed in the opposite direction the grizzly had gone. Mrs. Walberg groaned as if she were in pain. Mr. Walberg kept shaking his head and muttering. Gunther was in a daze. Alice was crying. So was her ma. Her pa looked to be in shock.

Clara felt strange, as if part of her were numb. She barely noticed when trees closed around them. Or the brush that plucked at her dress as her ma hurried her deeper in to a boulder half as big as their cabin had been back home.

"This will do," her pa said, putting his back to it.

"That infernal demon won't be able to get at us from behind."

Clara sat when her ma told her to. Alice plopped down, as well.

Gunther went on standing and quietly crying.

"This is horrible!" Mr. Walberg said.

"What did we do to deserve this?" Mrs. Walberg said.

"Deserve?" her pa said angrily. "Put the blame where it belongs. On that damn bear!"

"Language, Charles," her ma said.

"Oh, hell," her pa said.

Her ma sank down and placed her arms about her knees and buried her face in them. "My sweet Jacob!" she said, and wept.

Her pa put a hand on her ma's shoulder and said softly, "I know, dearest. I know."

"What I want to know," Mrs. Walberg said, "is what do we do? We have lost everything! We have no food! No other clothes! All our tools! Our belongings! Everything is gone!"

Clara stared off through the trees. The twin fires reminded her of bonfires back home, when everyone got together to eat and have fun. There was nothing fun about this.

"Our blankets! Our chest of drawers! Our quilts! My china!" Mrs. Walberg went on.

"Freida, stop," Mr. Walberg said.

She didn't. "My mother's clasp that I treasured so! The rattle our children used when they were little! The recipes my mother passed on to me from her mother! Your father's pipe! Your mother's shawl! So many heirlooms!"

"Freida, please," Mr. Walberg said.

Mrs. Walberg finally fell silent except for low sniffles.

Alice surprised Clara by pushing to her feet and shaking her fists at the adults. "What is the matter with all of you?" she just about screamed.

Their ma looked up and their pa turned.

"Alice Marie," her ma said.

"Calm yourself," their pa said.

"Calm?" Alice said, and now she shook her fists toward the burning wagons. "Hermann and Jacob are dead! Everything we own is going up in flames! We're stranded in the wilds, and all Mrs. Walberg can think to do is cry over her recipes?"

"Alice," her ma said again.

"That's not what matters," Alice said, tears streaking her cheeks. "What matters is that godawful bear! Do you think it will stop with Jacob? Do you think it will go away and leave us be? Do you?"

"Otto and I have our rifles," her pa said.

"What good did they do when the bear took Jacob?" Alice said. "Both of you shot at it. Did it drop dead? No. You might as well have used peashooters!"

"Enough, daughter," their ma said. "You're on the verge of becoming hysterical."

"Verge?" Alice said, and laughed as Clara never heard her laugh before. A high-pitched, keening sort of laugh that caused goosebumps to break out on Clara's skin. "Aren't you listening, mother? As sure as you're sitting there, that bear will come back! It will take another of us! And keep on taking us until there are none of us left!"

"You don't know that," their pa said.

Alice moved to him and placed her hands on his chest. "Pa, it followed us! From way down below, it trailed us all the way here! It's hunting us like a fox or a coyote hunts a rabbit! It's hunting us and killing us whenever it pleases and there's not a blessed thing we can do to stop it!"

Her pa scowled.

"We have to leave this valley, pa," Alice pressed on. "Leave here and now! Put as much distance as we can between that grizzly and us! If we can make it to the prairie we can head out after the wagon train."

"Wander off in the dark?" her pa said.

"That grizzly doesn't care if it's night or day!" Alice said. "It can kill us whenever it wants!"

"Even if I agreed to leave, it wouldn't be until morning. It's too great a risk?"

"We're at risk now!" Alice said, and stepped back, shaking her head. "Do what you want. But I'll be switched if I'm going to stay and wait to be slaughtered!"

"There's strength in numbers," their ma said.

"You go off alone, the bear will run you down, easy," their pa said.

"It's better than sitting here doing nothing!" Alice said.

Clara wished they would stop fighting. It upset her terribly. When her sister wheeled and strode past her, she jumped up and took hold of Alice's wrist. "No!"

"Let go," Alice said, tugging.

"We're a family!" Clara said. "We should stick

together."

"Sister! Heed me!" Alice said. She thrust her other hand at Clara, seeking to push her away, but Clara clung fast.

"I won't lose you too," Clara said.

"I swear," Alice said. "Release me or I'll wallop you!"

"You'll do no such thing," their ma said.

"Your sister loves you," their pa said. "She knows you're making a mistake."

Alice gave voice to a very unladylike growl and stamped a food. "My family! Simpletons! You'll get me killed and yourselves, besides."

"That will be quite enough," their ma said.

"The bear," Gunther said, and pointed.

He said it so quietly, it was a wonder anyone heard him. Yet they all did. And they all turned.

The grizzly had emerged near the wagons. Its muzzle was red with blood and it was licking its lips.

Their ma moaned.

Bathed in light as bright as day, the bear stared at the burning wagons. First one, then the other, ponderously swiveling its enormous head.

"Don't anyone make a sound!" Mr. Walberg cautioned.

"It knows where we are," Alice said.

"Be quiet anyway," their ma said.

Clara thought about Jacob. The griz hadn't had time to eat him. Not all of him. Or did bears only eat parts of people?

"Will you look at that!" Mrs. Walberg said.

The grizzly was lying down. Resting its forepaws

flat, it lowered its chin and went on staring at the burning wagons.

"What is it doing?" Mrs. Walberg whispered.

"It likes watching the flames," Mr. Walberg said. "Much as we like to watch fireworks."

"That's preposterous," Mrs. Walberg said.

"You see it with your own eyes," Mr. Walberg said.

Clara saw, and shuddered. She had never heard of a bear like this. Never heard of an animal like this.

It was the scariest thing in her whole life.

Chapter 22

Nate King woke up with his senses fully alert. Early on in his life as a Mountain Man, he trained himself so that the moment he became aware he was waking up, he leaped out of the vale of sleep, as it were, with his mind as sharp as it could be.

Only in the safety of his cabin did he let himself awaken slowly, almost luxuriously.

Now Nate sat up and saw that the sun was an hour into the sky. An hour he could have used hurrying to the aid of the settlers.

His bay was the reason he had stopped. It needed rest badly. So as much as he chafed at the delay, he had stopped late the previous night.

Nate stood and stretched. He donned his possibles bag and reclaimed his Hawken from where it had lain on the ground next to him.

In less than five minutes he was under way. Pemmican from his parfleche sufficed for breakfast. He would dearly love coffee but he didn't have the time to spare.

He thought of Winona and Bright Rainbow and hoped they were all right.

He thought of Sapariche and hoped the old warrior was recovering.

He thought of the Gordons and the Walbergs and

prayed he was needlessly concerned and the grizzly had let them be.

Something inside of him told him that wasn't the case. An instinct, perhaps. Or his years of dealing with grizzlies like this one.

No, Nate corrected himself. Never, ever had he encountered a bear like this. A bear that liked to rip its victims, human or otherwise, into chunks and pieces.

A bear that apparently killed for the sheer pleasure of killing.

A rare trait in animals, most people would say.

Nate knew of a fox that killed eleven chickens in a coop, and only ate one. He'd heard tell of a cougar that killed seven sheep and didn't eat any. There was a coyote that killed an entire litter of kittens, and the mother besides, and left them lying where they fell.

So no, an animal killing for killing's sake wasn't as rare as most people believed.

The knowledge did him little good. A killer was a killer. Who cared why? The important thing was to stop the grizzly before it did to the settlers as that coyote had done to the kittens.

He could only pray he was in time to help.

Clara's eyelids were so heavy they felt like big rocks. She wanted to sleep. Wanted to so much. Instead she forced her legs to work. To take yet another step.

"Are you all right, little one?" her ma asked.

"Yes," Clara lied. She was far from all right. She was exhausted. Hungry. Thirsty. Her legs hurt from all the walking. Her arms and legs were scratched up.

"We have to keep going," she heard her pa say. "We

have to put as much distance behind us as we can."

It was the middle of the morning. They had been walking since not long after both covered wagons caught fire. Her pa's doing. He insisted they get out of there before the grizzly tired of watching the flames and came after them.

Mrs. Walberg said. "As if it will really make a difference how far we go."

"Freida," Mr. Walberg said. "Please."

"Don't please me," Mrs. Walberg said. "I have lost my oldest son."

"*We* lost him," Mr. Walberg said. "And Charles and Elizabeth have lost theirs, as well. Stop reminding us."

Mrs. Walberg plodded along with a shawl over her head and her eyes moist. "I will never stop reminding you. How does someone forget such a thing?"

They were out of the valley. Out of the woods, too. Clara was glad about that. All night she had been pricked and nicked by brush and the like.

Strung out in a long line, they were descending a hill that was mostly grass. Now and then boulders loomed.

Her pa was in the lead. Alice came next. Then Clara's ma and Clara. Behind her was Mrs. Walberg and Gunther. Bringing up the rear was Mr. Walberg.

They were all bone tired. Clara could see it in their faces and how they moved.

Alice surprised Clara by slowing and waiting for her to catch up and then falling into step next to her. "How are you faring, sis?"

"All right," Clara lied again.

"I still can't believe about Jacob," Alice said softly.

Clara fought down an urge to cry.

"This is a nightmare," Alice said. "We never should have left South Carolina."

"Alice," their ma said. "You're not helping matters, either."

"I don't care," Alice said. "I don't care about anything any more."

"You don't mean that," their ma said.

"Jacob was a good brother. Hermann was always nice to me. You want me to forget them just like that?" Alice snapped her fingers.

"We will mourn them properly when we are safe," their ma said.

Clara hated their bickering. She hated the grizzly. She hated the wilderness. Above all, she hated that she couldn't lie down and sleep.

"You need to know something, ma," Alice said as she trudged along. "If we make it out of this alive, I'm not staying in these mountains. I'm not going on to Oregon Country. I'm going back East. Back to the States. Where it's safe."

"Nowhere is truly safe, daughter."

"South Carolina is. South Carolina didn't have grizzlies. South Carolina didn't have hostiles. In South Carolina we never worried about our next meal. We had clothes on our backs and a roof over our head. We have kin there. I make it out, that's where I'm bound." Alice placed her hand on Clara's shoulder. "And the little one can come with me if she wants."

"I'm your mother," their ma said. "I decide where the two of you go."

"Not anymore," Alice said.

Clara was looking at the ground when a pair of boots appeared. She stopped so suddenly, she nearly tripped.

Her pa had stopped and turned. He was mad. His face was red like that time Jacob left a lantern where one of their cows bumped it and nearly burned their barn down. "That will be quite enough!" he said harshly to Alice. "You will apologize to your mother. You will apologize to her this instant."

"Charles," their ma said.

"No daughter of ours talks to us like she just did to you," their pa said. "Such behavior is not to be tolerated."

Alice squared her slender shoulders and regarded their father defiantly.

"I'm waiting," their pa said.

Clara was amazed at how bold her sister was being. They were never, ever to sass their folks. It was what her pa once called a cardinal rule.

"I'm sorry I was gruff to ma," Alice said. "But I don't apologize for the rest." She took a deep breath. "I won't stay in these mountains! Nor anywhere in this horrid West! I just won't! And you can't make me! Not after what happened to Jacob! Not after poor Hermann!"

"I am the head of this family," their pa said.

"We don't have any say?" Alice responded. "We're your slaves who always have to do your bidding?"

"Daughter," their ma said.

"I was serious when I told you I don't care," Alice said. "I like being alive, ma. I like breathing. I aim to go on for as long as the Good Lord will let me."

Their pa took a step so that his face was bent over hers. "How dare you?" he said. "When have I ever treated you like a slave? Your grandfather has slaves. They work from dawn until dusk and live in little shacks and never have decent clothes. I wanted no part of that. Which is why I struck off on my own. Which is why I've always treated you as I wished my pa had treated me."

"She didn't mean a real slave," their ma said.

"Don't defend her," their pa said. He wasn't done with Alice. "When have I ever worked you to death? When have I ever made you do something you didn't want to do? Other than chores and the like?"

"You made us come here," Alice said petulantly.

"For the good of the whole family," their pa said. "For a new start. For somewhere we could be completely free. Somewhere there aren't any slaves and never will be."

"Pa...," Alice said.

"You want to leave these mountains?" their pa said. "Fine. I do too. I want to go on to Oregon and begin a new life. It will be hard. We have barely anything to our name now. But if we remember we're a family and stick together we will be back on our feet before we know it."

Clara would like to believe him. He was always good at painting a rosy future. But they were a long way from Oregon and she was so tired and hungry and thirsty, the idea of Oregon was like a dream that would never come true.

"Everyone,! Gunther unexpectedly called out, breaking his day-long silence.

"What is it, son?" Mr. Walberg asked.

Gunther had turned and was gazing back up the mountain. He swallowed and his Adam's-apple bobbed, and he raised an arm and pointed.

No, no, no, no, no, Clara thought. She knew what she would see before she turned. She tried to brace herself but after Jacob and Hermann, fear washed over her like ice-cold water from a bucket on a freezing winter's day.

Far up where the forest gave way to grass, a huge brown shape had appeared. No more than a brown blob, it left no doubt as to it's identity.

"The grizzly!" Mrs. Walberg exclaimed.

"Or the buffalo," Mr. Walberg said."

"Why would the buffalo follow us?" Mrs. Walberg said. "Why would it stand there staring like that."

"It is too far away to tell what it is doing," Mr. Walberg said.

"It's the bear," Clara's pa said. "I can feel it in my bones."

So did Clara. The grizzly was after them again. She supposed she should be grateful it was taking its sweet time and not barreling down on them like a runaway buggy.

"Look there!" Mr. Walberg said. "All of you are worried for no reason."

The brown shape had turned and was disappearing back into the trees. It didn't move so much as melt.

"You see?" Mr. Walberg said. "It is returning to the valley. We are safe until we are out of the foothills."

"Otto, you dreamer," Mrs. Walberg said. "You are trying to put yourself in that monster's shoes. But you can not think like it does. Or even like a dog or a cat. People aren't animals."

"It will leave us be," Mr. Walberg insisted.

Clara's pa gestured. "Whether it will or it won't, keep going. Daylight is wasting. And keep your eyes peeled for a spot where can stop for the night. Somewhere the bear can't get at us."

"Is there such a place anywhere on God's green earth?" Mrs. Walberg said.

Clara would like to know the answer to that question herself.

Chapter 23

They had been hiking for about half an hour when Gunther cried out again.

The brown shape was back. Larger, but still distant. It grew even larger until after a while there was no question what it was.

"The grizzly!" Mrs. Walberg said. "I knew it! The thing is following us."

"The word is stalking," Clara's pa said. "We're being stalked."

"Who cares what we call it?" her ma said. "The question is, what are we going to do?"

Clara shut them out. She was so weary she couldn't keep her eyes open much longer. They drooped, and she didn't try. A comforting cushion of emptiness yawned and without hesitation she sank into it, only to be jerked back to reality by her mother shaking her shoulders.

"Clara Jane! Wake up, child! You nearly keeled over!"

Dazedly, Clara blinked and mumbled, "I'm so tired, ma."

"Look at her, Charles," her ma said. "Look at her sister and the boy. We must stop and rest or they'll give out on us before sunset."

"I will not," Alice said.

"I've been looking for a spot to make a stand," their pa said.

Clara's ma let go of her and straightened.

"Look harder."

As they tramped on, Clara had to force her legs to take each step. Alice moved up with their ma and soon thereafter Gunther glued himself to her side.

"You look as tired as I am," he said.

"Tireder," Clara said.

Gunther glanced around, then said quietly, "I'm worried sick."

"Who isn't?"

"I mean it. We're all going to die."

A flush of anger lent Clara a flicker of new energy. "Don't talk like that. You heard my pa. So long as we stick together we can lick that thing."

"Do you really think so?" Gunther said, and answered his own question. "No. No one does. Our parents say it so we won't be afraid. But I am. I've never been more afraid in my life."

Clara couldn't say what compelled her to reach out and take his hand. "Keep those notions to yourself. You'll just upset everybody." As he had upset her.

"I'm sorry," Gunther said. "I can't help it. Not after Hermann."

"I lost my brother too," Clara reminded him. The memory was seared into her forever.

Behind them Mrs. Walberg said, "That's enough about them. Gunther, you should know better. This poor girl doesn't want to be reminded. You shouldn't think of it either."

"How can I not?" Gunther said.

Mrs. Walberg was going to say more but she fell silent when Clara's pa let out a whoop and veered toward a break in the ground.

"A gully, by God!" her pa said.

Clara didn't see what he was so excited about. To her it looked as if a storm had washed out part of the hill. A gap not much wider than their pantry had sides that rose higher than her pa. The near end sloped a bit but then it straightened. Lengthwise, it was about as long as their chicken coop used to be.

"You're joshing," her ma said.

"There's enough room for all of us," her pa said. "And the bear can't get at us except from the front."

"It could drop right in on top of us."

"Be serious. You saw how big it is. It would become wedged fast. No bear would be that dumb."

"I don't know, Charles. I fear we might trap ourselves."

"I've seen nowhere else, Elizabeth."

"We could push on."

"As tired as the kids are? Or you and Freida are, for that matter?"

"We can hold out as long as you men."

Her pa looked back up the mountain.

So did Clara.

The bear was close enough that its ears stood out and the black of its nose was visible against the lighter brown of its muzzle. It came on a brisk walk, its gazed fixed unwaveringly on them.

"Into the gully," her pa called out. "The little ones first, then Alice and you ladies."

Clara's ma put her hands on Clara's shoulders and

moved her to the opening. "In your go."

"Ma," Clara said uncertainly.

"Do as your father tells you," her ma said.

"You too, Gunther," Mrs. Walberg said.

Gunther went first, giving Clara a glance that told her he was as unhappy about the situation as she was.

Clara followed but haltingly. The walls of earth rose to blot out much of the sky and the sun. It was like being in the grain bin in the barn, only worse, because she could always climb out of the bin. But climbing the near sheer sides of the gully would be impossible.

She became even more upset when Alice and then her ma and Mrs. Walberg came in after her, completely blocking the only way out. They were penned in like so many sheep and from somewhere she remembered a phrase she heard, something about 'to the slaughter'.

"Ma," Clara said again.

"Hush."

Mr. Walberg had backed in and now her pa was following suit. They stood where it was widest, side by side, with their rifles to their shoulders.

"When it comes we shoot together," her pa said. "Go for the head."

"I have heard that bear skulls are very thick," Mr. Walberg said.

"Shoot it in the eye then."

"I will try Charles but I am not that good a shot."

Clara heard all this but she could barely see them because of the others in-between. "Ma," she said a third time.

"Honest to goodness," her ma said. "Give it a rest, child. Not a sound. Not so much as a peep, you hear?"

Clara tried to see how close the bear was by rising on her toes but she was much too short. She gave a hop and then another. She still couldn't see.

"Here it comes!" Mrs. Walberg said.

"We shouldn't be in here," Gunther said to Clara.

Her pa said, "Not yet, Otto! It's not in range."

"I want it dead so much," Mr. Walberg said.

So did Clara. She wanted the bear dead more than she ever wanted anything in her entire life. She broke out in a sweat and looked up at the sky to try and keep from feeling closed in.

"What is it doing?" Mr. Walberg said. "Why has it stopped and is just standing there looking at us?"

Clara desperately wished she could see. She bent right. She bent left. She hunkered and did the same. All she saw were legs and the backs of those in front of her.

"Look how it stays just out of rifle range," her pa remarked.

"So?" Mr. Walberg said.

"How would it know to do that unless it has been shot at before?"

"Maybe it has. By other settlers. By trappers. Do the Indians have guns?"

"I hear some do," her pa said. "But even bears that have been shot at don't often do what that one is doing."

"It is a devil!" Mrs. Walberg declared.

"Don't talk like that," Mr. Walberg said.

"Well, it is."

"Think of the children."

"They know it the same as I do. Only a devil would follow us so far. Only a devil would rip our sons to pieces. Only a devil would attack our camp and destroy our wagons and all of our possessions."

"It's just a bear," her pa said.

"Charles, I like you, you are a friend, but you fool yourself," Mrs. Walberg said. "I have come to the conclusion you do not see the world as it is...." She stopped. "Wait. Look. What is it doing now?"

Clara tried to squeeze past Alice but there wasn't room.

"It's pacing back and forth," her pa said.

"What for? To taunt us?" Mr. Walberg said.

"Animals pace all the time," her pa said. "I've seen I don't know how many dogs and cats pace. When a dog wants to go out or a cat is hungry."

"It has stopped. Look!"

Clara was so frustrated at not being able to see, she could scream.

"It's up on two legs!" her ma said.

"My Lord!" Mr. Walberg said. "How huge it is! It can kill us without half trying."

"Now who isn't thinking of the children?" Mrs. Walberg said.

Clara heard a loud gasp from possibly her ma and a squeal of fright from Mrs. Walberg.

"It is down on all fours again," Mr. Walberg said.

Her pa said grimly, "Here it comes!"

Clara nearly jumped out of her skin when a hand fell on her shoulder. Gunther was as pale as a sheet and shaking like a leaf.

"We are doomed!" he whispered.

"Stop it," Clara said.

A rifle boomed, the sound so loud in the narrow

space of the gully that Clara thought her eardrums had burst. But no.

Mr. Walberg uttered a sort of low cry.

"You fired too soon!" her pa said. "And you missed!"

"I couldn't have!"

"Reload!" her pa cried. "For the love of heaven don't just stand there!"

"Shoot! Shoot!" Mrs. Walberg yelled.

"What are you waiting for?" Clara's ma shouted.

"I want to be sure!" her pa said.

Another blast filled the gully and a small cloud of smoke rose to join that from Mr. Walberg's rifle.

"Reload! Reload!" their ma hollered.

"Oh God!" Alice said.

A third shot cracked, followed immediately by the thud-thud-thud of heavy paws and a roar that made the shots seem puny by comparison. Mrs. Walberg screamed. A loud thump preceded Alice being flung back against Clara so hard, they both fell, Clara slamming into Gunther and taking him down with her. There were shouts and curses and another scream.

Clara was able to push clear of her sister and rise up high enough to behold a nightmare made real.

Everyone was down. Her pa, her ma, both Walbergs. All flat on their backs, bowled over by the impact of the massive grizzly plowing into them. Her pa had been knocked against her ma and they were tangled up with Mrs. Walberg.

Mr. Walberg was closest to the bear.

"No! No!" he shrieked.

The grizzly had taken Mr. Walberg's left ankle in

its mouth. A crunch, and a screech, and the next thing, the bear was dragging Mr. Walberg away from the gully, Mr. Walberg yelling and struggling and kicking with his other foot. He clawed at the ground to no avail. Looking back, he wailed, "Freida!"

Mrs. Walberg made it to her feet. She barreled out of the gully, breaking free of Clara's ma, who tried to stop her.

"Freida, don't!"

Mr. Walberg was a good distance away and still being dragged.

Mrs. Walberg ran after him.

Clara's pa was up and he went to give chase but her ma grabbed him with both arms.

"No, Charles! There's nothing you can do!"

"I have my pistols!" her pa said. To Clara's astonishment, he gave her ma a powerful shove and raced to aid the Walberg's.

Chapter 24

Clara clutched her hair and screamed. She was certain the bear would kill her pa just as it had killed her brother. It tore her heart in half to see him rush so recklessly to his own death.

She was barely aware when her mother and Alice each took hold of a hand and pulled her to her feet. Barely aware that her mother also took Gunther's hand.

Out in the open Mr. Walberg was still fighting, still kicking with his free leg and punching and shouting.

The grizzly ignored the blows and the yells and went on dragging him. It wasn't in any great hurry.

Mrs. Walberg had almost caught up to them. She was screaming her husband's name over and over and over.

Clara's pa ran flat out. He was shouting for Mrs. Walberg to stop. She didn't listen.

The bear stopped, though. It stopped and let go of Mr. Walberg's leg and raised its enormous head and looked at Mrs. Walberg.

Mr. Walberg rolled onto his stomach and frantically crawled toward his wife while at the same time motioning for her to go back. He was hollering, "No, Freida! No, Freida!"

Clara's mom and Alice pulled her and Gunther out of the gully, and stopped.

"What do we do, ma?" Alice said.

"Charles!" their ma yelled.

Their pa had almost caught up to Mrs. Walberg.

The grizzly broke into motion. In a lumbering jog it ran past Mr. Walberg, who glanced up in alarm, toward Mrs. Walberg and Clara's pa.

Mr. Walberg's look changed to horror. "Freida! Run! Run! It is coming after you!"

Mrs. Walberg abruptly halted and stood with her hands clasped to her bosom. For some reason she raised her head to the sky.

"What is she doing?" Alice said in dismay.

"Praying," their ma said, then screeched, "Charles!"

Their pa slowed and glanced back. When he turned toward Mrs. Walberg, the bear had reached her.

"Freida!" Mr. Walberg wailed.

The bear rose onto its hind legs, rearing so high, it towered over her like a giant over a child. Her face was still tilted to the sky. She didn't scream. She didn't shrink away or collapse in fear. The bear looked toward Clara's pa, then down at Mrs. Walberg.

Mr. Walberg tried to rise but his leg wouldn't support him and he fell. "Freida!"

The grizzly's head dipped and just-like-that, Mrs. Walberg's head disappeared into its mouth. Even as far away as Clara was, she heard a loud crunch. Blood spurted, and Mrs. Walberg's shook and trembled and her arms went limp.

"Freida!" Mr. Walberg cried.

The bear opened its mouth and Mrs. Walberg's body fell to the grass and convulsed.

The grizzly looked at Clara's pa.

Clara was sure it was going to attack him. It probably would have except that Mr. Walberg let out another wail and the bear swung toward him instead.

"Charles!" their ma shouted.

Her pa drew a pistol from under his belt.

"Please, Charles! Please!"

Clara didn't understand what her ma was saying please for.

Mr. Walberg had reached down and was tugging at the pistol under his own belt but it was stuck and wouldn't come loose. The bear reached him and he glanced up.

Clara's pa was moving to one side, maybe trying for a clear shot at the bear's vitals.

The grizzly uttered a strange snuffing sound. It raised a front leg and stomped its huge paw down much as a person would stomp a bug. Only the grizzly stomped on Mr. Walberg's face. A bone cracked loudly, or his spine did, and his head was driven into the ground with such force, it split open and blood and part of his brains and other fluids burst out.

"Charles! For the love of God!" her ma yelled.

At last their pa heeded. He turned and began running back, slowly at first but faster as he went.

The grizzly didn't come after him. Bending, it licked at Mr. Walberg's head, at the blood and the brains.

"I'm going to be sick," Alice said.

"Like the devil you are!" their ma said. "Hold it in."

Their pa reached them. Wearing the oddest expression, his eyes wet, he said, "They're gone! Both of them!"

Their ma nodded.

"There was nothing I could do."

"I know."

The grizzly had its muzzle pressed to Mr. Walberg's head and its tongue kept flicking, in and out, lapping at the inside of the skull as if it were so much pudding.

"We must run, Charles," their ma said.

"Yes," their pa said. But he didn't move.

"We must get away before it comes after us."

"Yes," their pa said.

Clara's ma let go of her hand and stepped to their pa and slapped him. Not hard, but enough that he blinked.

"Come out of it!"

"I am," he said, and cleared his throat. "I am," he said louder.

"Let's not waste a second!"

"No, no, of course not."

Clara's ma took hold of her and Gunther and the five of them ran around the gully and on down the hill to where the going was easier.

No one said anything. Clara figured they were in shock, the same as her. They came to a belt of woods and threaded in among the trees, her ma in the lead, her pa at the back.

"We're all of us dead," Alice said bleakly.

"Don't talk like that," their ma said.

"We're dead and you know it, ma."

"I will smack you like I did your father."

Alice fell quiet and they hiked until Clara was on the verge of collapsing once more.

In a clearing ringed by small pines their ma stopped

and let go of her and said, "Everyone rest."

Gunther took a couple more steps, sank to his knees, and bowed his head.

Clara did the same next to him. "I'm sorry about your folks."

Gunther was crying.

"I liked them," Clara said.

"I don't want to talk about it," Gunther said.

"Sorry."

"Hermann. Ma. Pa. I am alone now. There is only me."

Clara didn't know what to say.

"I have no one," Gunther said, and sobbed.

"You have us now, boy," Clara's pa said, draping a hand on Gunther's shoulder. "My wife and I will look after you the same as if you were our own. You have my word on that."

"If we live long enough," her sister said.

"Alice, so help me," their ma said.

Clara was tired of it, too. "Sister! Stop!"

"Don't face the truth if you want," Alice said. "But don't expect me not to."

Their pa said, "Which way were we running?"

"How's that again?" their ma said.

"I lost track," their pa said. "We should have been going east but by the sun I think we drifted to the south or maybe southeast."

"What difference does it make?"

"Not much, I suppose. But it will take us a longer to reach the prairie."

"If we reach it," Alice said.

Clara was thinking of the bear, and of something

else. "Did you reload your rifle, pa?"

"What?" He raised it and sort of grinned. "By heaven, I forgot in all the excitement. Thank you for reminding me."

"A gun won't do any good," Alice said.

"That is the last straw," their ma said.

Their pa set to reloading. "As soon as all of you are up to it, we'll keep on the move. The bear will be busy a while so we can put some distance between it and us."

"Busy?" their ma said. Then, "Oh."

"If it comes after us," their pa said as he slid the ramrod out, "we'll be smarter next time. We'll stick near trees."

"Trees?" Alice said.

"Bears can climb when they're little but not when they're full grown. They're too heavy. That griz in particular. We find trees it can't push over and climb them so we are out of its reach."

"And what? Sit in the trees until we starve to death?" Alice said.

"No, daughter. I will shoot it and could get lucky."

"Our luck has been in short supply for a good while now," Alice said.

Their ma scowled. "What has gotten into you?"

"I'm at the end of my rope, ma," Alice said forlornly. "I've tried to be brave and keep my spirits up. But the Walbergs are all gone except for Gunther and our wagons are gone and everything we own is gone and we are alone in this godforsaken wilderness and I am tired of it. Tired of running. Tired of being afraid. Tired of being in dread of the end. We were foolish to think we could make a go of it here. These mountains aren't South Carolina. They're a savage place. A horrible place. A place where people like us don't belong. We're peaceable. We like to get along with everyone and everything. These mountains don't care. The wilderness doesn't care. The wilderness tears at you until there is nothing left except your bones."

Clara never heard her sister say so much at one time.

"That's morbid," their ma said.

"It's true," Alice said.

"No one ever told you this would be easy," their pa said.

Alice gave a laugh that was more akin to a bark. "Easy? Jacob is dead, pa? My only brother. Your only son. He's dead and we will never be together again and it's all this wilderness's fault."

"The grizzly is to blame," their pa said. "Nothing else. Stop making more of it than there is."

"That bear is part of the wilderness," Alice refused to let it drop. "And it's not the only thing out to kill us. Are you forgetting the hostiles? The rattlesnakes and the wolves and the mountain lions and who knows what else? Are you forgetting what they told us about the winters? Yet you brought us here anyway. You thought you could make a go of it in a place where you had no idea what it would take to do that."

Their ma clenched her fists. "That will be quite enough. This time I mean it."

Alice lowered his chin to her chest, her hair falling over her face.

"Leave her be, Elizabeth," their pa said. "She has every right to be upset. And you know what? She's right. Partly. With Otto and Freida gone, and our wagons, we can't hope to survive. Nor would it make much sense to push on to Oregon Country. I'm thinking we should head back East. Like she mentioned earlier, there we have kin who can help us. We're heading home, everyone."

Clara's heart leaped at the news.

At that moment, off in the woods, a loud crashing arose.

"The bear!" Alice exclaimed.

Her pa raised his rifle to shoot.

Chapter 25

Nate King's bay was lathered and weary when he reached the valley where the settlers were starting their new life.

It was close to sunset and Nate imagined the settlers settling down to their supper. He wouldn't mind a hot meal and some coffee. He would warn them about the grizzly and stick around to protect them should the need arise.

Holding his exhausted horse to a slow walk, Nate entered the valley.

Almost immediately he caught a whiff of a burnt smell. Not the normal smell of a campfire, though. This was different.

Drawing rein, Nate straightened and sniffed. There it was again.

Resting the stock of his Hawken on his thigh, Nate tapped his heels to his mount. He wound through a last tract of timber and ahead stretched the valley floor. To his left the stream gurgled. Here the smell was particularly strong.

Nate gazed up the valley but didn't see the covered wagons. Or any of the settlers.

He warily advanced.

Soon the entire length of the valley opened out before him, mired in shadow.

Still no wagons.

Nate didn't know what to make of it. The wagons were too big for the settlers to have taken them into the woods unless a lot of trees were cleared first. And why would the settlers bother when the wagons were fine in the open?

He scanned the ground and spied the ruts made by the wagons when they entered the valley.

There were no ones.

No sign at all the wagons went back out.

Strangely, he did spy flattened grass and several partial hoof prints which suggested some of the oxen and horses had headed for the open end of the valley not that long ago.

Nate rode on.

The burnt smell grew worse.

He saw no one. He didn't hear voices. Given that both families had young children, that was troubling. Children loved to play and made a lot of noise doing so.

Nate raised his head as high as he could. In the area where he had last seen the wagons was a broad black swath littered with debris.

"No," Nate said to himself.

Among the debris were a stove and a rake head and a shovel, the metal blackened, the handles gone. All that was left of the wagon wheels were iron bands once fastened to the rims. The bonnets were gone except for the metal bows. Bolts for the tongue and the box were mixed with metal household items such as pots and pans and utensils and the like. Some partially melted.

Both wagons, quite clearly, had burned to the

ground.

Bewildered, Nate swung down. He couldn't begin to imagine what caused the disaster. Had a lit lantern broke and spewed its contents? Had one of the children been responsible? Whatever the cause, why hadn't the adults moved the other wagon? Or had both caught fire at the same time?

He went to rove in search of tracks and stopped cold.

There, clearly imprinted in the ash, was the track of a huge grizzly. Of its forepaw.

Nate turned in a circle.

There were others, front and hind prints, showing the bear had roved about.

Nate was anxious to find more sign but dark was descending and both he and his horse were tuckered out. He led the bay over to where the woods lined the stream and set about making a fire. Once it was crackling, he cradled his Hawken and walked about shouting the names of the settlers.

Once, high in the mountains, a wolf howled.

Later, coyotes yipped.

An owl voiced the perennial question of its kind.

But no one answered him. Not so much as a faint cry from anywhere.

Returning to the fire, Nate sat, opened his parfleche, and took out some pemmican. As he ate he pondered.

Either the families were dead or they were no longer in the valley.

He inclined to the latter.

There were no bodies amid the debris or anywhere

else. He supposed he could conduct a wider search in the morning. But if he was right and the settlers were gone, the wisest recourse was to light out after them.

He must do what he could to save them. Particularly the children. He couldn't get them out of his head.

Children were special. They were the heart of a family. The promise of a future. They came before all else.

Nate had devoted himself to his. To being the best father that he could be. He didn't always measure up, not in his own estimation. But he did the best he could in any given circumstance, which was the most anyone could hope for.

He tried to guess how long the settlers had been gone. If they were on foot---and the tracks suggested they were---he stood a good chance of overtaking them fairly quickly.

Nate gazed at the stars that sparkled like so many gems. Usually, after a rough day, the spectacle soothed him. Not tonight. He was too worried. And too tired.

He added a piece of branch to the fire and eased onto his back with his Hawken at his side and his right hand on a pistol.

The image of little Clara popped into his head and he smiled. She was always so friendly. So kind. He hoped---he prayed---that she and her family were all right.

In the wilds there was no predicting.

The wilderness could be downright brutal.

Icy fright gripped Clara. She was deathly afraid the

grizzly had returned to kill another of them. Her hand flew to her throat.

She saw her pa press his rifle to his shoulder. Knew he was about to shoot.

The next instant she spied the cause of the racket in the brush.

Clara screamed. Not in fear for her life. For the life of another. She screamed as she had never screamed before, a piercing, "Pa! No! It's Mr. King!"

Someone else had recognized him. Her ma, who flew at her pa and knocked the barrel of his rifle down just as it went off. The lead ball meant for the Mountain Man blasted into the ground, kicking up dirt and not a few pines needles.

Mr. King hauled on his reins and brought his big horse to a stop an arm's-length from Clara. His horse looked about ready to collapse. Mr. King looked awful tired, too.

He smiled wearily and leaned forward in his saddle and said in that deep voice of his, "Please to see you're still alive, little one."

"Mr. King!" Clara exclaimed.

"Told you before," he said. "Call me Nate."

Her ma came up, and Alice too, Gunther trailing after them.

"Praise the Lord!" her ma said.

Nate King stared at her pa. He didn't seem mad that her pa had almost shot him. All he said was, "Close."

Her pa swallowed and nodded and wiped his brow with his sleeve. "I was thinking of my family."

"Know the feeling," Nate said.

"Thought you were the grizzly." Her pa bowed his head and took deep breaths.

Nate dismounted. "Thank you, ma'am, for knocking his rifle down."

"I saw it was you first, is all," her ma said.

Alice rose onto her toes and peered past him. "Where are Mrs. King and Bright Rainbow?"

"Off helping someone" Nate said.

"I wish they had come," Alice said.

Nate said, "Given what I saw at your camp and on the way here, I don't need to ask where the rest of you are, do I?"

"The bear got them," Clara said. "All of them except us."

"Reckoned as much," Nate said.

"My brother. Mr. and Mrs. Walberg. Their biggest boy."

Nate's expression was grim.

"Our wagons burned."

Nate gave the top of her head a friendly pat. "You're holding up well, all things considered."

"I'm scared," Clara admitted.

"We all are," her ma said.

Alice nodded.

Her pa was reloading and glancing nervously about. "We never know when it will show up. It could be out there watching us."

"Probably is," Nate said.

"Help us, King, please," her pa said.

"It's why I'm here."

"Where are Mrs. King and Bright Rainbow again?" Alice asked.

"Taking care of one of those Utes you met," Nate said. "The griz got the other two."

"My God," her pa said.

Nate let his reins drop and strode past Clara to Gunther. "Sorry about your folks and your brother."

Gunther's bottom lip trembled and the corners of his eyes grew damp.

"Let it out if you have to," Nate said. "There's no shame in a man crying when he has reason to."

Gunther shook his head.

"What do we do, Mr. King?" her ma said. "That bear won't leave us be. How do we get out of this alive?"

"There's only one way," Nate said. "We kill the griz."

"I shot it," her pa said. "I'm pretty sure I hit it. But it didn't go down."

"Meriwether Lewis liked to say that grizzlies are hard to die," Nate said.

"Lord, was he right. I had no idea they were so fierce. Even after the stories I've heard."

"We can kill it if we work together," Nate said.

"How confident you sound," her ma said as if that surprised her.

"You don't get something done by thinking you can't do it," Nate said.

Clara laughed.

"This is hardly a lark, daughter," her ma said.

Her pa said to Nate, "The Indians must call you Grizzly Killer for a reason. Tell me what to do and I'll do it."

"It won't be easy."

"I trust your judgement."

"First we find somewhere safe for your missus and the younguns," Nate said. "Their lives matter more than ours."

"I beg to differ," Clara's ma said. "My husband and you must live through this too, else what's the point?"

Her pa said, "Have you ever heard tell of a bear like this one before? That stalks people mile after mile?"

"No," Nate said.

"Why does it do it?" her pa said. "Just to eat us?"

"I think this bear enjoys it."

"Enjoys stalking and killing?"

Nate nodded.

"Well, hell," her pa said.

Chapter 26

Clara was happy as could be that the Nate King had shown up. So was everyone else. She could tell.

From what she gathered, he had killed more than a few grizzlies before. Which was why the Indians called him Grizzly Killer.

As tired as she was, Clara didn't mind that he was pushing them to find a safe place before the sun went down. He had taken charge as naturally as anything and her pa and ma didn't mind. Astride his big horse, he followed behind, keeping watch for the bear.

Clara and her family and Gunther were hurrying the best they could. Her legs felt wooden. But she could be hanged if she would give up.

As near as Clara could tell, they were about halfway down the foothills. Far below lay the prairie, a sea of grass that stretched to the eastern horizon.

To the west half the sun was gone. Soon it would dip below the high peaks and plunge the world into darkness.

Gunther came up beside her. He was still terribly sad over his folks and his brother but he had perked up a little after Mr. King joined them. "Do you think he can save us?" he asked, his voice low so only she heard.

"Mr. King?"

"Who else?"

"I do, and that's a fact," Clara said.

"I wish he had showed up sooner," Gunther said. "My father and mother might be alive. Hermann too."

"Mr. King told us he came as fast as he could."

Gunther looked at her and opened his mouth and closed it again.

"What?" Clara said. She thought he was going to say something about Mr. King or his parents but he surprised her, to put it mildly.

"Would you like me for a brother?"

Clara didn't know what to say.

"I've lost my family. I'm alone," Gunther said forlornly. "You lost your brother." He paused. "I need a new family and you need a brother so why not? Would you ask your father and mother for me? I know your father wants to send me back to live with relatives but I don't want to go all the way back. I want to stay with you and your family." He was so choked with emotion that he stopped and sniffled.

"Oh my," Clara said.

"I would like you as a sister," Gunther said. "You're always nice. And I'd always be nice to you."

"I can ask my ma," Clara said. "It wouldn't be up to me."

"Would you? Please?"

"Sure," Clara said, and smiled when he clasped her hand and gently squeezed.

They were nearing the bottom of a hill. Before them spread a wide bench of land covered in short grass. There were no trees, no large boulders.

Her pa raised an arm and called out for them to stop. "Is this what you told me to keep any eye out for?"

he said to Nate King.

Nate tapped his heels to his horse and rode past them. "It will have to do. The sun is almost gone and we have to be ready when it is."

Her ma said, "It's so open."

"That's the point," Nate said.

Clara would like nothing better than to lie down and go to sleep but it wasn't to be. All of them hurried to the closest trees and gathered up armloads of downed limbs, the men breaking the large ones, and brought the firewood back.

Pretty soon they had two growing piles where Nate King wanted them to be. They kept adding and adding until Clara thought her arms would fall off.

The piles were about ten feet apart. Nate had her family and Gunther gather between them. Then he and her pa built fires about a hop and a skip from each pile so all they had to do to keep the fires burning was toss a piece of wood into each.

Her pa was next to one pile, her ma next to the other.

Stars were sparkling when everything was ready.

They had to sit close to each other. Clara was between Alice and Gunther.

Nate swung down and brought his horse between the piles and held onto the reins.

The fires were comforting. Crackling noisily, they spread light in a wide circle.

"What good will this do?" Alice spoke. "The bear can get at us from any direction."

"Must you carp so?" their ma said.

"We'll see it coming," Nate King said. "Or my

horse will hear it or smell it and let us know. We should have enough warning that we can get off some shots."

"Should," Alice said.

"Honestly," their ma said.

Clara thought it a grand idea. Taking cover in the gully hadn't done them any good. In the woods the bear could pounce out of nowhere. Here, it couldn't do that. "Mr. King will save us," she confidently predicted. "You'll see."

"I hope so," Alice said.

Nate hoped so, too.

His Hawken and his pistols were loaded. He had his tomahawk and his Bowie. The fires, and his bay, should be sufficient to keep the griz from taking them by surprise.

Even so, even with forewarning, stopping the bear, bringing it down, would take luck more than anything. That, or the hand of Providence.

Hunkered by the fire with his rifle across his lap and the reins wrapped around his left wrist, Nate scanned the night as he had been doing for hours.

The Gordon clan and young Gunther had turned in.

Next to him, the bay dozed standing up.

Nate let it. The horse was worn and needed the rest. Even so, its senses were such that a strong scent or the pad of a huge paw would bring it instantly awake and alert him.

At least, that was what Nate was counting on.

Mr. and Mrs. Walberg, Hermann, Jacob, had all endured horrible ends. He would spare the rest that if he could.

He gazed at the children and the oldest daughter and then at the parents. All were deep in the heavy slumber of exhaustion. Waking them would take some doing.

Charles and Elizabeth had tried to stay awake to help keep watch. She succumbed first. Then it was Charles who slipped into dreamland, his cheek resting on the barrel of his rifle.

Safeguarding them was squarely on Nate's shoulders.

Lordy, he was tired, too.

Fortunately, he'd gotten some sleep the night before so he should be able to stay awake until dawn.

Should be.

Stifling a yawn, Nate shook his head to clear a few cobwebs. He noticed that the fire to his right was burning low so he added part of a limb. When the flames rose higher he sat back.

High on the mountain a wolf howled, a lonesome lament that made Nate think of the woman he loved. He would give anything to know that she was all right. She should be. She could handle herself as well as anyone.

Nate yawned and gave his head another toss. He would love some coffee. Say, a pot or two. The notion made him smile, a smile that instantly died when his horse gave a slight snort and raised its head with its ears pricked.

Nate was instantly alert.

His horse was staring toward the last hill they had descended. Something was up there. Was it the grizzly?

Unfurling, Nate stood. He pressed the stock of his Hawken to his shoulder and curled his thumb around the hammer. He must be ready to shoot in the blink of an eye.

The bay's nostrils flared and it moved its head slightly.

Nate firmed his hold on the reins. He mustn't let the horse run off.

Little Clara muttered something in her sleep and rolled over. Her arm fell across Gunther, who mumbled and turned away from her.

Annoyed that he let himself be distracted, Nate looked up.

Something was on the slope above the bench. No more than a vague shape silhouetted against the slightly brighter background of the night, it was enormous. Too huge to be a deer. Too huge to be anything other than a buffalo or a bear. And as Nate had recently witnessed, buffalo made a lot more noise than this thing had done.

The bay stared right at it.

"Look who it is," Nate said to himself. He didn't shoot. Without a clear shot at the grizzly's vitals he would only wound it. Which was the worst thing he could do.

Wounded grizzlies were viciousness incarnate.

The bear didn't move. It didn't do anything but stand there, staring.

The bay gave a snort of agitation and tugged at the reins.

Nate held fast. He heard a loud sniff, and another. Not from his horse. From the shape on the hill. The temptation to shoot, to try and drive it off, was so strong, he had to will himself not to do it.

A spot of shine appeared. The firelight reflecting off....what? There was only one, not two as there would be if it were the bear's eyes. And the spot was lower than Nate imagined the eyes should be.

The shine increased, becoming a sort of triangle.

Yet another loud sniff sounded.

Nate realized the shine was the grizzly's nose. The tip of its muzzle, to be exact. Why it went on sniffing puzzled him. It already knew their scent.

More of the muzzle appeared along with a suggestion of twin pinpoints. Its eyes.

Nate took a bead on the left eye. If the bear charged he would fire. A head shot, given how thick bear skulls were, was out of the question. The same with its chest. A throat shot might kill but he didn't have one. So it would be the eye.

The twin pinpoints became the size of small coins.

The griz was closer.

Nate felt goose bumps break out from his head to his toes. He feared he wouldn't be able to stop it and those innocently asleep at his feet would pay the price.

The bay tugged harder.

Nate made up his mind. Any closer, and the griz would be on them before he got off a shot. He steadied his Hawken and girded himself to fire.

The gleaming coins became larger still.

Nate's finger was commencing to tighten when Clara Gordon sat up and rubbed her eyes with her knuckles.

"Stay down!" Nate whispered.

"Mr. King?" Clara said sleepily, and looked about

her in confusion.

"Go back to sleep," Nate said. Her movement might provoke an attack.

He glanced toward the hill.

The shape was gone.

Chapter 27

To say that Nate was tired was an understatement. He was weary to his core. He had stayed up the rest of night.

A bright pink band was etching the eastern horizon, heralding the beginning of a new day.

Nate stood and stretched, feeling the muscles on his arms and shoulders ripple.

The grizzly hadn't returned. Why, Nate couldn't say.

Clearly, it was stalking the settlers. Clearly, it intended to slay each and every one. Equally clearly, and proof yet again, this was a griz like few others.

Nate had more experience with the great bears than most. Since his first days on the frontier, it had been his misfortune to encounter them more often than most. Invariably he sought to leave them be and go his own way.

The grizzlies weren't always so disposed. Again and again he had been forced to kill or be killed.

But those bears were normal. They hadn't stalked him for days on end.

There was an exception, a grizzly known as Scar. It had haunted the vicinity of a particular Ute village, returning again and again to slay members of that particular band.

STALKED

No one ever heard of such a thing.

The brutal killings went on until the Utes appealed to Nate for help and he put an end to the monster's reign of terror.

It turned out that years ago a hunting party slew Scar's mother. One of the warriors tried to kill Scar, too. Then only a cub, the young bear lived but bore the mark of the warrior's tomahawk. From that day on, Scar hated the Utes with a hatred that went beyond anything Nate ever heard of.

This new bear reminded Nate of Scar. It was similarly obsessed. Except that this bear's obsession was to slay anything and everything with a viciousness that defied belief.

If Nate was to keep the Gordon family and young Gunther alive, he must get them out of there. Out of the foothills. Away from the bear's territory.

His wisest recourse was to rejoin Winona and head for Bent's Fort. There, the Gordons would be safe. They could find passage to wherever they wanted to go, whether it be on to Oregon or back East.

He added wood to the fire. No one else was awake yet. He decided to let them go on sleeping. They would need the rest for what was to come.

In due course Elizabeth Gordon roused. She sat up quickly and glanced around as if fearful of being attacked. When she saw Nate she relaxed and ran a hand through her hair. "Morning," she whispered.

Nate nodded and swept his gaze over the woods and the slopes above.

"It left us be?" Elizabeth said in surprise.

"For the time being," Nate said.

Elizabeth looked at the others, then rose to her knees and bent toward him. "I don't want to scare the children but I need to know the truth so answer me true."

"Of course."

"There is no way to escape that bear, is there? It will keep after us until it kills us, yes?"

"It will try," Nate said.

"What do you suggest? I'll go along with whatever you say." Elizabeth went on before he could respond. "My husband might have other ideas and as much as I love him, he is out of his depth. He's done his best and it hasn't been enough. To be frank, Mr. King, he's no match for this creature, although I would never say so to his face. It would hurt him terribly." She paused. "So what do you think we should do?"

Nate told her about Bent's Fort.

Elizabeth nodded. "Then that's how it will be. I very much doubt Charles will object but if he does I'll side with you and hopefully he will see reason."

Nate didn't see why the man would. Standing, he walked about to stretch his legs and get his blood flowing. He gazed to the east and admired the beautiful display of the rising sun, then to the north where a red hawk was taking wing, then to the west at the towering peaks that thrust like so many lances at the brightening blue of the sky.

Finally he turned to the south, and froze.

For there, standing full in the open on the crest of an adjoining hill, was the grizzly. Staring back at him.

Nate's first instinct was to raise his Hawken but the range was much too far. Cradling it, he returned the stare.

This wasn't mere chance, Nate reflected. The grizzly wanted them to see it. The bear wanted them to know it was there. Watching. Waiting. Biding its time until its next attack.

"What are you....?" Elizabeth Gordon said, and gasped. Rising, she came to his side. "Why is it just standing there like that? What do we do?"

"Nothing," Nate said.

"Be honest with me," Elizabeth said. "Have you ever known a bear to behave this way?"

Nate shook his head.

"It will shadow us, won't it?" Elizabeth said, her voice starting to rise.

"Stay calm," Nate said.

"How can I?" Elizabeth said, clenching her fists so hard her knuckles were white.

"Ma?" Clara said, sitting up and yawning. "What's happening?"

Elizabeth hurried to her.

Nate turned toward the hill again---and the grizzly was gone. He had half a mind to go after it but checked the impulse. It would be rash. And foolish. For all he knew, the grizzly wanted to draw him away so it could kill more of the family. That seemed preposterous. No bear was so cruelly devious. And yet, how else to explain this grizzly's behavior?

The rest were stirring. Alice was next to rise. She absently smoothed her dress, looking completely miserable.

Gunther's eyes were pools of fear.

Only Charles came to life with a smile. A forced

smile, no doubt. He clapped Gunther on the back and gave each of his daughter's a squeeze and his wife a big hug.

Nate had to hand it to him. The man was trying his best to keep his family's spirits up.

"Is there anything for breakfast?" Alice asked. "I'm starved."

"I have pemmican left," Nate said, and proceeded to hand out a piece to each of them. He didn't mention seeing the griz. Elizabeth Gordon didn't mention it, either. Why scare the little ones more than they already were?

Alice didn't seem to like her pemmican very much. She kept grimacing as she chewed. When she was done, she said, "This is it? This is all we get?"

"I'll kill something for the supper pot," Nate said. "Count on it."

"Go all day without anything else to eat?" Alice complained.

"You really need to stop this," Elizabeth said.

"Stop what?" Alice said.

To nip an argument in the bud, Nate raised his arms to get their attention. "Everyone listen. We stick close together from here on out. Clara and Gunther will ride my horse---."

"Why them?" Alice interrupted. "Why can't we take turns?"

"They're the youngest and can't walk as fast as we can and they'll tire sooner," Nate explained. "And we need to keep moving no matter what."

"I get tired too," Alice said.

"Alice!" Charles said.

"I'll lead the horse. He's used to me," Nate said. "Charles, you come behind. Elizabeth on one side, Alice on the other." He paused. "You see the bear, any sign of it at all, you let me know right away."

"What do I do if it attacks?" Alice said. "Throw rocks?"

Nate turned to her father. "You have two pistols."

"One is mine," Charles said. "The other was Otto's."

"Give one to your missus. The other to Alice. Everyone needs to be armed."

"Me too?" Clara said.

"Sorry, young one," Nate said. He was holding onto his own weapons.

They got under way.

The day was beautiful, not a cloud in the bright blue sky. Wildlife was everywhere. A rabbit bounded off. Squirrels scampered. Several does flicked their tails.

"Maybe the grizzly is gone," Elizabeth commented at one point. "Otherwise the other animals wouldn't be about."

Not necessarily, Nate thought to himself. The wild things were accustomed to bears. The deer and the like fought shy of them but didn't go into craven hiding. Once a bear had passed them by, they went about their usual lives.

He stuck to the open.

Forest, he gave a wide berth. Clusters of boulders, too. Anywhere the griz might lie low in ambush.

Hardly anyone said a word. The little ones were tight-lipped with worry. Alice was in a funk. Charles was keeping an eye on their rear. Elizabeth appeared disheartened.

The morning passed uneventfully.

Below, the foothills undulated like so many rolling green and brown waves to blend into the prairie.

At midday Nate called a halt in an open area where the griz couldn't take them unawares. He perched on a small boulder with his rifle across his legs to keep watch while the others rested.

"I'm so thirsty I could drink a river," Alice said.

"I know of a stream," Nate said. "It's where we'll camp tonight."

"Are you worried about Mrs. King and Bright Rainbow?" Clara asked.

"Some," Nate admitted. Not as worried as he would be if he weren't absolutely certain the grizzly was shadowing them and not his wife.

"I don't see how you've lived out here all the years you have," Elizabeth said. "I never realized how dangerous it is."

"It's not as if we run into grizzlies or hostiles every single day," Nate said. "Whole months and even years can go by without much happening."

Gunther, who hadn't spoken in hours, said angrily, "I hate it here! Hate it! Hate it! Hate it! I wish we'd never come!"

Elizabeth placed a hand on his arm. "There, there. You have us now."

"No!" Gunther said, and shook her hand off. "I want my mother! My father! My brother!"

Elizabeth tried to embrace him but he pushed away, his eyes filling with tears.

"I can't stand this anymore!"

"Stay calm, boy," Charles said.

Gunther stared at him, his face twitching. Suddenly he burst into tears, shot to his feet, and raced away bawling at the top of his lungs.

"Gunther, no!" Elizabeth cried.

"Gunther!" Clara echoed.

Charles started to rise, saying, "I'll go after him."

Nate was already on his feet. "No. Stay and guard your family." He broke into a run, moving faster when he saw that Gunther was pulling ahead. "Gunther! Stop!"

The boy didn't heed.

Not fifty feet from Gunther's flying form was a belt of woodland, oaks and small pines mostly. He had one hand over his face and the other flung in front of him and was bawling louder than ever.

Nate poured on the speed.

Chapter 28

For all they knew the grizzly might be lurking in the woods, waiting its chance to pounce.

"Gunther!" Nate shouted.

It was doubtful the boy could hear him over the bawling.

Nate vaulted a small boulder. He came down on his left heel, which slipped out from under him. Before he could stop himself, he fell, pinwheeling his arms in a vain effort to stay upright. He landed flat on his back and immediately regained his feet.

By then Gunther was in the woods.

Clenching his jaw in frustration, Nate continued his pursuit. He reached the trees and saw the boy still running and bawling.

"Gunther!"

Again the boy kept on going and disappeared around a thicket.

Nate sped around the same thicket and took several long strides and stopped dead.

Gunther was nowhere to be seen.

Bewildered, Nate looked right and left. He heard a low wail and sniffling.

Darting to a pine, he poked his head around.

Crouched over, Gunther was crying his heart out. He had his hands to his ears as if to shut out the world and everything in it.

Nate went closer and was about to touch the boy's shoulder but caught himself. It might be best to let Gunther cry himself out. Sometimes that helped.

He didn't like being separated from the Gordons, though. Granted, the should be able to spot the grizzly coming from a long way off and he would hear the shots and could race to their aid. But still.

Gunther was crying up a storm. The loss of his mother and father and brother had ravaged his poor heart and he was letting all his emotions out.

Nate would do the same were he to lose any of those nearest and dearest.

Leaning his shoulder against the pine, Nate waited for the boy to stop.

Weary, he closed his eyes and rubbed them.

Just as from out past the woods a scream pierced the air.

"What's keeping them?" Clara's father said.

Her ma responded, "I can still hear the boy crying. so they can't have gone that far."

"I still don't like it," her pa said.

They were all watching the woods to the south.

Clara was keenly anxious for Mr. King to return. When he was with them she felt safer.

"The boy deserves a good talking to," her pa said.

"Now, now, Charles," her ma said. "We can't hardly blame him. Not after all he's been through."

"Even so."

Clara didn't blame Gunther at all. She blamed the grizzly. Every awful and terrible thing that had happened was the bear's fault. She wished she were an adult and had a rifle and came across it so she could shoot it her own self.

Nate King's bay nickered.

Clara wasn't paying much attention to it. Then it nickered a second time and she looked and saw its head was raised and its ears pricked. She wondered what it heard.

The bay turned its head and looked behind them.

Clara's stomach fluttered as a terrible feeling came over her. A feeling so certain, so sure, she wasn't at all surprised when she turned her own head and there was the bear.

Somehow, the grizzly had come up on them as silently as anything. Right out in the open. Even with their backs turned she was amazed they hadn't heard it or sensed it.

Uttering a loud whinny, Nate King's horse wheeled and broke into a gallop, fleeing past Clara and her ma and pa and Alice, heading down the hill toward the distant prairie as if its hindquarters were on fire.

"What in the world?" her ma blurted.

"Where's that fool horse going?" her pa said.

Clara was too terrified to speak. The grizzly's eyes were locked on hers and it was as if the bear were willing her to stand there motionless. She tried to break free of the spell but her mind wouldn't work as it should.

Alice turned and shrieked.

Clara gave a start. The spell was broken. She backpedaled and tripped and landed on her bottom.

The grizzly suddenly reared on its hind legs. It was

enormous, the most gigantic thing in Creation.

A paw rose and Clara knew it was about to strike and there was nothing she could do.

That was when Alice darted between Clara and the bear. "No!" she screeched. "Leave her be!"

In astonishment Clara saw her sister hit the bear with her fists. The blows had no effect, except that for a few moments the grizzly seemed to pause, as if it, too, was as surprised as Clara at her sister's act.

"Run!" Clara yelled, afraid the beast's huge paw would descend and strike her sister down.

Instead, the grizzly lunged, its mouth gaping wide. How something so immense could move so swiftly was beyond Clara's understanding.

The result was hideous.

The bear's massive jaws closed on Alice's left shoulder. She screamed as its fangs sheered deep into her flesh, her scream rising to a keening peak as bone crunched and blood spurted.

"Alice!" their ma cried.

Their pa sprang in close and jammed the muzzle of his rifle into the grizzly's chest. He yelled, "Let go of her!" and fired.

The blast wasn't nearly as loud as Clara thought it would be. Muffled by the bear's bulk, the shot was more of a *pop* than a sharp explosive *crack*.

Given that the muzzle was gouged into the bear's body, Clara looked to see it stagger and spurt blood of its own. That close up, the lead ball surely penetrated deep. To her consternation, the grizzly didn't show any sign it was stricken.

As casually as a dog might pick up a stick and trot

off, the grizzly lifted Alice off her feet, turned, and started toward forest to the north.

"Noooooo!" Clara wailed, scrambling to her feet.

Her pa was frantically reloading.

Her ma ran after the bear, crying Alice's name.

"Elizabeth!" her pa shouted. He stopped reloading, cast down his rifle, drew one of his pistols, and ran after her.

Clara ran, too. She didn't want to. She just did it. The bear had her sister.

Alice hung limp in the bear's mouth. Scarlet was spreading across her shoulder and down the back of her dress.

"Alice! Alice! Alice!" her ma bawled.

"Elizabeth, stop!" her pa yelled.

Tears formed in Clara's eyes and she blinked them away.

The grizzly was moving faster as if anxious to get to cover and feed. Or so Clara thought until once again the bear did the unforeseen. Suddenly stopping, it spun and faced its pursuers.

Alice's right arm moved at if beckoning them. Whether of her own volition or because of the bear was impossible to say.

Clara took it as a sign her sister was still alive. "Alice!" she wailed.

Her ma had hiked her dress and was running faster than Clara ever saw her run, and she didn't seem to care that she was getting ever closer to the bear.

"Elizabeth, please!" their pa shouted.

The grizzly let go of Alice. It simply opened its mouth and she plopped to the ground in a crimson-drenched heap.

Clara had another awful feeling. A certainty that the bear was going to attack her ma. Incredibly, though, the monster just stood there watching her approach. Maybe it would turn and go, Clara prayed. Maybe it had done enough and wasn't interested in eating any of them. Maybe.

Her ma reached Alice. Ignoring the bear, she dropped to her knees and pulled Alice into her arms. Her ma was crying.

"Elizabeth!" their pa bawled..

The grizzly took a single step. That was all it needed.

Clara's ma didn't glance up. All she did was hold Alice tighter and rock back and forth.

Clara's blood was ice in her veins. She knew the grizzly was going to kill her ma. It would take a miracle not to happen.

Then her pa abruptly stopped, extended his arm, and cocked his pistol. He was aiming as best as he could and in another couple of heartbeats he stroked the trigger. Smoke spewed at the retort.

The grizzly's head was bent, and was about to bite. It was a big target. A target even a poor shot could hit.

Jerking its head to one side, the bear let out a loud roar. When it straightened, a red furrow was visible high on its brow.

The ball had struck but hadn't penetrated. Deflected by the bear's thick skull, all it did was draw blood.

The grizzly started toward her pa.

Clara stopped and called out to him.

Her pa was drawing his other pistol from under his belt. This time he aimed with both hands. Calmly, cooly, he thumbed back the hammer, aimed and fired. Whether he scored was impossible to say. The grizzly didn't stop. It didn't slow.

Whirling, her pa flew back toward his rifle. He saw Clara and veered. Before she could say a word, he scooped her up and resumed running.

"Be still!" he said.

Over his shoulder Clara saw the bear closing on them. She had the impression it wasn't running as fast as it could.

"Damn me! Damn me! Damn me!" her pa said.

Clara had no idea why.

They were almost to the rifle when he practically heaved her from him. She landed on her shoulder and cried out from the pain. Rolling, she came up into a crouch.

Her pa scooped up his rifle and went to reload before the grizzly reached him.

He wasn't going to make it.

Chapter 29

Clara never wanted to leave South Carolina. It was her home. Where she had lived all her life. To be uprooted like a tree and taken off whether she wanted to go or not saddened her beyond measure.

She hid her feelings, for the most part. For the sake of her folks and her sister and brother she kept her sorrow to herself.

She never much liked the wagon train. Never much liked living out of a wagon, period. To her it was just plain silly to leave a perfectly fine cabin to go clattering off across the prairie in a wooden box covered by canvas.

She had put up with it, though. Again, as much for her family as for the fact that if she complained, her ma wouldn't take it kindly.

The Rocky Mountains filled her with awe. She liked them, at first. They were spectacular to gaze upon. So high. So majestic.

The valley that Mr. King led them to soothed her worries somewhat. It was pleasant. Peaceful.

But always in the background hovered the bear. The mountains, and the valley, became the nightmare she secretly feared they might.

Now her brother was gone and Mr. and Mrs. Walberg were gone and Hermann was dead and maybe her sister and in less than a minute the grizzly would reach her father and he would be gone, too.

Clara screamed.

Her pa was tugging at the ramrod as if it were jammed but he wasn't looking at his rifle. He was staring at the charging grizzly. And wearing the strangest expression. Almost as if he were in some sort of trance. Or maybe it was amazement at his impending doom.

The bear was almost on him when a rifle boomed somewhere to Clara's rear. She distinctly saw blood spurt from the grizzly's neck close to its throat. Since none of the other shots had much effect she didn't expect this one to, either.

But it did.

With an agility that belied its size, the grizzly swung to one side, missing her pa by inches. Her pa stood rooted as the bear pounded to the east faster than a man could sprint.

It was leaving! Clara realized. That last shot had hurt it and it was running away!

Her pa still gaped.

Her ma still cradled Alice.

Clara turned.

Nate King was reloading faster than her pa ever could. Jerking his Hawken to his shoulder, he sighted on the fleeing bear.

Behind him, a flicker of hope on his face, was Gunther.

The Mountain Man fired.

He scored, too, because the grizzly broke stride but instantly recovered and resumed its headlong escape with tufts of grass spewed in its wake.

The last Clara saw of it, the monster disappeared over the rim of the next slope.

Nate King started after it but apparently changed his mind and ran toward her, saying, "Are you all right, girl?"

Clara nodded.

Nate glanced at her pa and said, "Keep loading!" Then he was past both of them, making for her ma and Alice.

Clara made for them too.

"Wait!" her pa said.

Clara paid him no mind. She was too worried.

Her ma was cradling Alice and sobbing. She jerked away when Nate hunkered and put a hand on her shoulder. He said something and she shook her head.

Clara reached them in time to hear him say, "We need to take a look. I can't tell how bad it is with you holding her like that."

Her ma shook her head again.

Setting his rifle down, Nate tried to loosen her ma's grip but her ma stubbornly clung fast.

"Please, Mrs. Gordon," Nate said.

"Not my oldest girl!" her ma said. "Not her too!"

"We don't know as she is," Nate said gently. "Please." Once more he sought to loosen her ma's grip on Alice.

"Ma!" Clara cried. "Let him!"

Her ma looked at her, a look of such sorrow and misery and horror that Clara's heart was wrenched to where it nearly burst. Clara went up to her and put an arm around her neck and hugged her.

"It's me, ma. Let Mr. King look."

Ever so slowly, her ma let her arms droop.

Alice sank into Mr. King's.

Clara tried to see but her ma buried her face in Clara's shoulder and commenced to wail. To Clara it felt strange. As if her ma were the child and and she was the adult.

"I am so sorry," Mr. King said softly.

Her ma dipped her forehead to Clara's leg and cried and cried.

Clara finally saw.

Alice was gone. Her eyes were open but they were empty of life. Not empty of emotion, though. They seemed to show the shock she experienced at the moment of dying. The side of her neck and shoulder were a ruin. A large chunk was missing. The bleeding had stopped, probably because there wasn't any blood left. Alice's dress was soaked clear down to her waist, so wet it dripped red drops.

"Dear Lord, no!" her pa gasped.

Clara hadn't heard him come up. She was glad when he took her ma in his arms and tenderly eased her away. Her ma went on crying on his shoulder.

Clara looked at Mr. King and he looked at her.

"Let it out if you have to."

"No," Clara said. Strangely, she didn't feel the need. She dropped to her knees and placed a hand on Alice's arm and bowed her head, but that was all.

She had forgotten about Gunther and was reminded when he appeared at her elbow and sadly regarded Alice.

"Now your sister, too. That awful bear is going to

kill all of us."

"Enough of that kind of talk," Nate said more gruffly than he meant to, and inwardly winced when the boy turned away and broke out in more tears.

The mother continued to wail.

The father was silently weeping.

Only the girl was holding up. Possibly because she was all cried out.

Nate stood and moved away to let them grieve as they would. Only then did he realize his bay was gone. It must have run off. He roved in a circle, seeking sign, which was as plain as the nose on his face. His bay had fled east.

Nate stiffened.

So had the griz.

Initially, he figured the bear was fleeing pell-mell because he had wounded it. Was it coincidence, then, the grizzly went in the same direction as his horse? Or was the bear after it, intending to slay it as it had the one Sapariche told them about?

If so, this grizzly was devious beyond reason. Sinister in a way no other bear Nate ever confronted had proven to be.

Nate would dearly like to give chase. He couldn't stand the thought of his bay being torn to bits. But both horse and bear were a lot faster than he was and could go miles farther. By the time he caught up, if he did, it would be over.

Resting his Hawken's stock on the ground, Nate reloaded. A glance at the stricken family pierced him to his marrow. He had failed them yet again. Another of their loved ones was gone. Granted, he couldn't have let Gunther run off. Someone needed to fetch the boy back and he was best suited.

It struck him, then, that the grizzly must have waited until he went after the boy to attack the others.

"God in heaven," Nate said.

His early days in the mountains came to mind. His previous encounters with the lords of the Rockies were nothing like this. Then it was straightforward. The bears tried to kill him and he did his best to thwart them. Simple clashes. Man against beast.

This?

This was different.

This was.....evil.

Some folks might scoff. They might say a grizzly was a grizzly and nothing more. That he was making the bear out to be more malevolent than it could possibly be.

Perhaps.

Or did this grizzly kill for the sake of killing and nothing more? Did it revel in the gore and the blood? Was a bear capable of experiencing pleasure when it killed?

Nate frowned. He didn't know. The only aspect he could be certain of was that this particular grizzly wasn't going to stop attacking them until each and every one of them were dead.

A hand touched his and Nate almost jumped out of his skin.

"Mr. King?"

Nate swallowed and turned. "You should be with your ma and pa, Clara."

STALKED

The girl's dress was wet from her mother's tears and she picked at it with a finger. "They cry and they cry. There's nothing I can do."

"I am sorry for your loss," Nate said, wishing there was more he could say or do.

"She was trying to save me from the bear," Clara said. "She jumped right in front of it." Clara stopped, her voice breaking. "I never knew...."

"No need to talk about it if you don't want," Nate said.

"I never knew," Clara said quickly, "that she cared so much."

"She loved you. You were her sister."

Clara looked up, her eyes welling, her bottom lip quivering. Uttering a small groan, she sank to her knees, placed her hands over her face, and cried.

Nate rested his fingers on her shoulder but she shook them off, doubled over, and let her tears out in a torrent. Thinking she would like to be alone with her grief, he moved off a suitable space.

Gazing off down the mountain, he sought some sign of his bay or the grizzly.

"Mr. King?"

This time it was Gunther.

"What can I do for you?" Nate asked.

"We need to killl that bear."

"Couldn't agree more," Nate said.

"I've been thinking," Gunther said. "When we went fishing my father would bring worms."

Unsure what the boy was getting at, Nate nodded. "Worms are good for catching fish, yes."

"And my uncle, when he wants to shoot a deer, he

puts out a salt lick."

"That's one way," Nate said.

"Bait, they call it," Gunther said.

Nate thought he understood. "You're saying we should use bait to lure the grizzly in so we can kill it?"

Gunther nodded.

"A good idea," Nate said. "But we don't have bait we can use."

"There's one."

"What?"

"Me," Gunther said.

Chapter 30

The first thing that popped into Nate's head was that the boy couldn't be serious. One look at Gunther's expression proved he was.

"You can put me somewhere the bear will come," the boy went on. "You hide and when it shows, you shoot it."

"No," Nate said.

"Why not?"

Nate squatted so they were eye to eye. "Because I can't be sure of keeping the griz from getting to you. You saw what happened when I shot it a while ago. It didn't go down."

"Then Mr. Gordon and you both wait and both shoot."

"Again, no." Nate smiled to lessen the sting of being refused. "I admire you, though, for wanting to do it. You're braver than I was at your age."

"I'm not brave," Gunther said. "I just want the bear dead. It killed my father. My mother. My brother. I have no one. I'm all alone."

"You have your friends," Nate said with genuine affection. "I'm one of them."

Gunther wasn't satisfied. "You really won't use me as bait?"

"Not ever," Nate assured him.

Dejected, the boy bowed his head and turned away.

Nate unfolded and cradled his rifle and waited for the family to finish with their grief. He would have preferred to push on. They were wasting daylight.

With the bay gone, their best bet was to find Winona. She had horses and supplies and, best of all, she was handier with her Hawken than Charles Gordon with his, and tougher, besides.

Lord, Nate missed her. They had been together for decades. It would please him mightily were they together for decades more. She was wonderful, that woman. Even more wonderful was that fact that she had become as much of a part of him as, say, his own heart or soul. She was everything. And she often said that he was the same to her.

Giving his head a shake, Nate looked around. There was still no sign of the bear.

Charles Gordon was beside Elizabeth and they were holding one another.

Clara was on her feet and rubbing her face with her sleeve.

Gunther was by himself, staring in misery at the ground.

Nate went over to Charles and his wife. "I hate to intrude," he said. "But we need to see to burying your daughter so we can keep going."

Elizabeth stared dejectedly at Alice. "I'm not up to going anywhere."

"We have to," Nate insisted.

Charles coughed and nodded. "He's right, dear. We shouldn't linger. The bear might return."

"I don't care," Elizabeth said.

"Elizabeth, please," Charles said.

"I don't care, I tell you."

"We've already lost one son and one daughter. I don't want to lose any more of us."

"No."

Charles glanced at Nate and moved his shoulders as if to signify he had tried.

Nate wasn't willing to back down. "What about your youngest? Doesn't Clara matter?"

"Of course she does," Elizabeth said.

"Then we need to get here to safety," Nate said. "My wife will be looking for us. We join up with her, we have a chance."

"I hate this," Elizabeth said.

"I know," Charles said.

"Hate it, hate it, hate it."

Nate recollected Gunther saying the same thing a while back.

"There's nothing else we can do," Charles said.

To try and hurry things along, Nate said, "If you want I'll do the burying. You can wait until it's done and then say a few words."

"No. I'll help," Charles said. "She's my daughter."

"Our daughter," Elizabeth amended. "We'll both lend a hand."

Unfortunately they had nothing to dig with except their knives and Nate was loathe to blunt his in the hard-packed ground. He roved in search of suitable rocks with tapered ends and found several that would suffice.

Returning, he immediately set to digging by dropping onto his hands and knees and scooping at the earth.

"You want to bury her here?" Elizabeth said. "I would rather it was the forest." She gazed toward the woods. "There's shade and birds. It would be much more fitting."

"I suppose....," Charles began.

Nate reckoned it would add an hour or more to the burial. They would have to to carry the body, find a spot the mother liked. "Here is better."

"She's our daughter," Elizabeth said.

"She's gone," Nate said bluntly. "It doesn't matter to her where we plant her. What does matter is if that grizzly comes back. It's too much of a delay."

Elizabeth appealed to her husband. "Charles? Tell him it should be the forest."

"He has a point, dear," Charles said.

"Yet again!" Elizabeth muttered. Angrily pushing his hand off, she stood and folded her arms across her bosom. "Fine. You men do as you will. Clearly I have no say even though I'm her mother." Wheeling, she stalked away, the portrait of outrage.

"Perhaps....," Charles said.

"No," Nate said.

"What would it hurt, really?"

Nate nodded at Alice and then toward Clara.

"Oh." Charles slowly rose. "Let me go talk to her and then I'll help you dig."

"I can manage on my own," Nate said. "You keep an eye on them and an eye out for the bear. Make sure all your guns are loaded."

"You can count on me," Charles said, and trailed after his wife.

No, Nate couldn't, but he kept that to himself.

Selecting the best rock, he gouged at the ground as if the rock were a knife, digging and scraping. To make a hole large enough would take considerable time. Time they could ill afford.

He knuckled to the task. Slowly, painstakingly, he made progress. By his estimation the hole was half done when a pair of shadows fell across him. He looked up in surprise.

"Do you have a rock we can use?" Charles said.

"She's our daughter. We should help," Elizabeth said. She frowned. "I'm sorry about earlier. I was upset. You're right and I was wrong. Escaping the bear is more important than anything else."

With the three of them at it, the hole was soon wide enough and deep enough.

The heat of the day had Nate in a sweat. Moping his brow, he helped Charles carefully lower Alice's torn form.

"Hold," Elizabeth said, and proceeded to arrange the girl's dress and body so that Alice almost looked as if she were merely resting. "That's the best I can do."

Nate and Charles commenced to scooping dirt and didn't stop until they had formed a mound and tamped it down with their feet.

"There!" Charles said.

"We should say a few words," Elizabeth said. "Where's Clara?"

The girl was where Nate last saw her, gazing off down the foothills. She came when called, her head hung low.

"We're showing our last respects," Elizabeth said.

"Is there anything you would like to say?"

"She tried to save me," Clara said.

"That's all?" Elizabeth said.

"She was a good sister most of the time," Clara said.

"Clara Jane," Elizabeth said.

"I loved her very much."

Elizabeth softened and placed her arm around her youngest. "We all did."

Charles cleared his throat and began reciting the Lord's Prayer.

Nate bowed his head and reined in his impatience. He deemed it prudent to put as many miles as they could behind them before the sun went down. When Charles came to the end, he chimed in with an "Amen" and thought that was end of it. He was mistaken.

"Lord," Elizabeth said, raising her eyes skyward. "This was our oldest girl. She was precious beyond words. We ask that....."

Nate listened with half an ear. Something was pricking at him, a sense of unease, a feeling that things weren't as they should be. He looked at Charles and then at Clara and at Elizabeth and at the grave and he couldn't quite put his finger on what was bothering him.

Elizabeth apparently had a lot to say and wasn't in any hurry. Evidently she intended to recite the story of Alice's life from the moment she was born.

Nate could respect that. He loved his own offspring as much as anyone, and were he to lose them, he would be crushed. As heartbroken as little Gunther was over the deaths of his mother and father and brother.

Little Gunther.

Nate glanced up sharply and swivelled right and left. "Where is he?" he blurted.

In the act of telling about the time Alice first learned to sew and kept sticking herself with the needle, Elizabeth wasn't pleased. "I beg your pardon? We're in the middle of the service, such as it is."

"I don't see him," Nate said in rising alarm.

"Who?" Charles said.

"Gunther." Nate moved around the grave past them. "Where did he get to?"

"Gunther?" Elizabeth said.

"I wasn't paying attention to him," Charles said.

"He walked off," Clara said.

Nate and both parents turned to her, and Nate and Charles both said, "What?"

"He walked off by himself," Clara said. She pointed to the east. "That way."

"What were we doing?" Elizabeth said.

"Talking and digging," Clara said. "I told him not to but he wouldn't listen."

"You knew he was going and you didn't stop him?" Charles said.

"He said he was doing it for Mr. King."

Nate bent and gripped her arm. "How do you mean? Tell me his exact words."

"You're squeezing too hard," Clara said.

Easing his hold, Nate said, "Please. It's important. We have to get after him."

"His exact words?" Clara's brow furrowed. "He told me that if you wouldn't use him as bait, he would do it for you. He would use himself as bait and bring the bear to us so you could kill it."

"Dear God!" Elizabeth exclaimed.

"The boy will be torn to bits!" Charles said. He motioned at Nate. "Go on. Find him. We'll catch up."

As worried as Nate was, he shook his head. "We go together."

"But.....," Elizabeth got out.

"If we separate it could be just what the griz wants," Nate enlightened her. "It has to be all of us. Now. This very moment."

"He's right, dearest," Charles said.

Elizabeth cast a despairing glance at the grave. "When will this ordeal end?"

Chapter 31

Nate chafed at their slow pace.

Elizabeth was so devastated by Alice's death that she moved slower than usual and had to be helped along by Charles.

Clara trailed along behind until Nate told her to get ahead of her folks so she was between him and them.

Out in front, Nate held to a walk. Against his better judgement. They needed to find Gunther quickly. If the griz spotted him, the boy was a goner.

Nate kept hoping to come on his bay. But no. The horse might have run for miles.

By rights Nate should rove ahead of the others. He could cover the ground much more swiftly. He dared not leave them, though.

It was three lives versus one.

A terrible choice.

Cupping a hand to his mouth, Nate bellowed the boy's name as loudly as he could. Maybe luck would favor him. Maybe the boy would answer.

Except for the screech of a jay, the mountains were ominously silent.

Clara came alongside. "Did I do wrong in letting Gunther go? Are you mad at me for it?"

"I'm mad at me for not keeping an eye on him," Nate said.

"What if we don't find him?"

"We will."

"But what if we don't? What if the bear gets him or a mountain lion finds him or a wolf comes across him or he is bit by a rattlesnake or---."

Nate held up a hand to stop her. "I get the idea," he said with a smile to try and lighten her mood.

"Well? What if?"

"Fretting over what might be is pointless. If you have to, fret over what is and then make the best of it or change it to as it should be."

Clara was silent a bit, then said, "I hope we make it out. I hope we go back East and stay there the rest of our lives. I don't like it here." She paused. "I hope you don't mind my saying so."

"Why should I? I'm not you. People like different things."

"Why do you stay, Mr. King? Aren't you afraid for your family? For Mrs. King and Bright Rainbow and your other daughter and your boy?"

Nate shrugged. "I suppose a day doesn't go by that I don't worry about them some."

"Then why stay?"

Nate gestured at high peaks practically brushing a few white puffs of cloud. "This fits me. It fits them."

"Huh?"

"Places are like clothes. Some fit us. Some don't. In the mountains my family is free to live as they please. There's no one looking over our shoulders and telling us we need to do this or that. No government. No politicians. No busybodies."

"That's important?"

"To some of us," Nate said. "Besides, when you've lived here long enough, the dangers become part of your everyday life. You get used to them as you get used to most everything."

Clara gave a short laugh. "I could never get used to grizzlies no matter how long I lived here."

"It's not as if we run into one every day."

"Maybe so," Clara said. "But once in my whole life is enough for me. I bet I have bad dreams about Alice for the rest of my days."

Nate had nothing he could say to that. "Over time you don't have as many."

"How do you know?"

"I've had bad things happen. When it does, you pick yourself up and go on---." Nate stopped because the girl suddenly halted and pointed.

"Look yonder! There's Gunther!"

The next hill down was half as high. Its north side was a sheer sandstone cliff. Its south, forest. The west slope and most of the crest was grass. And there, at the summit, seated cross-legged with his back to them, was the small bent form of Gunther Walberg.

"What is he doing?" Clara said.

Nate thought he knew. "He's set himself out there as bait, just like he said he would. He's waiting for the grizzly to show and then he'll try leading it back to us so your pa and me can kill it."

"That's plumb crazy."

"Also very brave."

Nate guessed that the boy was about two hundred yards off. Once again he wanted to break into a run. Once again he held himself in check. He did say over his shoulder to Charles and Elizabeth, "We should hurry. There's the boy."

He picked up the pace but after only a short way he looked back to discover that both parents were falling behind. Largely because of Elizabeth. She moved like a stricken turtle, the shock of the loss of her oldest daughter having taken severe hold.

Charles was doing what he could to hasten her along.

Backpedaling, Nate added his arm to help propel her faster. Almost immediately Elizabeth stumbled and would have gone down if not for their hold.

"I'm sorry," Charles said, bobbing his chin at her.

"Can't be helped," Nate said.

Charles nodded toward Gunther. "We're so close. Give a yell and have him join us."

Why not? Nate thought, and hollered Gunther's name. Not once but three times.

Gunther just sat there. He didn't look up or around.

"What's gotten into him?" Charles said.

"He's trying to lure the bear in."

"He'll be killed like his parents and his brothers."

"They are why he's dong it."

Charles nodded again. "Go fetch him. I can manage with my wife."

"We're sticking together," Nate said.

"It's not that far," Charles said. "If the grizzly comes at us I'll delay it long enough for you to rush back and help."

"No."

"He's a small boy, for heaven's sake."

"Still no."

"I won't have him die on my family's behalf."

"It's his decision," Nate said.

"He's hardly mature enough to make a decision like that." Charles was losing his grip and hefted Elizabeth. "If you don't go, I will."

"No," Nate said. "You won't."

"What? You'll force me to stay?"

"If I have to."

Charles glanced at his wife. "If Elizabeth were in her right mind she would agree with me. That boy's life matters as much as ours. She would want you to go."

Nate didn't respond. He had already said his piece.

"I won't be ignored," Charles said.

"Keep helping with your wife."

"Are you going or not?"

Nate was about to say he wasn't when Clara gave a yell.

"I'll fetch him, pa!"

"Daughter! Wait!" Charles shouted.

"No!" Nate cried.

They both could have saved their breath.

Clara fairly flew. She was fast, that girl, and agile, and reminded Nate of a young doe bounding flat out.

Charles looked panic-struck. "Clara! Consarn you! Stop!"

The girl was intent on reaching Gunther, and nothing else.

"Hold onto your wife," Nate said, and was off and away. He disliked leaving them but Clara left him no choice.

Two lives behind him, two lives in front of him. And the two in front were children.

Clara began calling out to Gunther. As before, he acted as if he didn't hear her.

Nate concentrated on running and nothing but running. The Shoshones considered him fleet of foot but it had been many months since he ran so far, so fast, and he was huffing and puffing before he started up the slope.

Clara was already halfway to the crest, and to Gunther.

"Clara!" Nate tried yet again. To his relief she glanced down. "Wait for me!"

She continued running.

"We'll fetch him together!" Nate tried. "In case the griz is near!"

At last Clara slowed and then stopped. She didn't appear the least bit winded. "You should hurry, Mr. King."

As if Nate wasn't. He ascended in long strides, glad he didn't have to contend with trees and roots and boulders. He was breathing heavily when he caught up to her, and ashamed of himself. His stamina wasn't what it used to be.

"Are you all right?" Clara said.

"Never better," Nate said. "Come on."

They climbed the rest of the way.

Gunther hadn't moved. His head was bowed and his elbows were on his knees.

"Gunther!" Clara called out. "We're here for you!"

Nate was growing worried. Had something happened? Was the boy hurt? Or was it worse?

"Gunther!" Clara shrilly exclaimed.

At long last the boy raised his head and looked back.

Instead of smiling or greeting them, he waved them off, saying, "Hide and wait for the bear. It could show any time."

Nate reached his limit. Angrily striding forward, he barked,"On your feet! I told you not to use yourself as bait and you didn't listen. Now you've put all of us at risk."

Gunther placed a hand on the ground but he didn't rise. "Please let me do this!"

"Mr. King?" Clara said.

Nate was focused on the boy. "Stand up! You're to stay with the Gordons and me from here on out. And don't give me any guff."

"Mr. King?" Clara said again.

"Just a second," Nate said. Sliding a hand under Gunther's arm, he yanked him erect. "I appreciate what you're trying to do. I truly do. But you're going about it all wrong."

"I'm trying to help and you won't let me," Gunther said sorrowfully.

"Mr. King!" Clara shrieked, and stomped her foot.

Nate turned and started to say 'What?' but didn't have to.

The answer was at the edge of the forest, staring back back at him.

The grizzly.

"What do we do?" Clara gasped.

Gunther took several steps and shook a fist at it. "I hate you, bear! You're going to die now! Isn't he, Mr. King?"

Nate's mouth went dry.

Chapter 32

The grizzly didn't roar or rush to attack. All it did was take a couple of slow, ponderous steps and raise its muzzle and sniff a few times.

"What are you waiting for, Mr. King?" Gunther said. "Kill it! Kill it now!"

"Take Gunther and go," Nate said to Clara.

Her eyes widening, she stood riveted in horror.

"Did you hear me?" Nate said, sidling in front of her and the boy so he was between them and the bear. "Take his hand and run!"

"Run?" Clara said as if she thought she hadn't heard correctly.

"Go!"

"My pa says never to run from animals," Clara said. "They might attack."

Ordinarily Nate would agree with her father but this was no ordinary bear. It would kill her even if she stayed perfectly still. "Run anyway. I'll protect you." As best he could.

Clara hesitated.

"Get to your folks," Nate said, not taking his eyes off the grizzly. When she didn't move he gave her a slight push. "Now!" he commanded.

She went up to Gunther and grabbed his hand and tried to go but he dug in his heels.

"No!"

"We have to!" Clara said.

"I want to see Mr. King kill it!"

The grizzly was watching the children, giving no clue to its state of mind. Not that that was difficult to divine.

Suddenly wheeling, Nate took hold of Gunther by the scruff of his neck and forced the boy to take half a dozen quick, stumbling steps. "Run!"

Clara pulled on Gunther's arm and managed to keep him going.

Nate faced the bear.

The grizzly had been oddly still but now it reared upright. Gigantic in the bright light of the day, it spread its forelimbs with their huge paws tipped by inches-long claws.

A growl rumbled from its chest.

Nate raised his Hawken to his shoulder. This was it. Do or die. He refused to retreat. Even should the grizzly let him leave, it was bound to come after them.

He might never have a better opportunity.

The griz opened its maw and roared.

Nate took a careful bead, talking as he did. "Your kind and me go back a ways, bear. You've had it in for me from the start. I've lost count of how many times I've been attacked. And all I ever wanted was to be left alone to live my life in peace."

The grizzly cocked its head as if it were actually listening.

"So if this is my end, I'll go out doing what I've long been doing. Killing silvertips like you who think they can do as they please to everything and everyone."

The bear took a short step.

"They call me Grizzly Killer," Nate said. "You're about to find out why."

He fired. He went square for the chest, going for a heart shot. The ball might be deflected, in which case it might puncture a lung.

The grizzly swayed, tottered, and recovered.

Nate didn't bother trying to reload his rifle. The bear was too near.

Casting the Hawken to the grass, he drew both flintlocks and extended them, cocking the hammers. He stroked the trigger of the one in his right hand and had the satisfaction of seeing blood spurt from the bear's neck even as it dropped onto all fours.

Nate aimed his second pistol.

The grizzly charged.

This time Nate went for an eye. Sometimes the lead tore through into the brain pan. His pistol blasted and smoke spewed.

Reacting as if it had been kicked by a mule, the bear lurched and twisted but came on again as fast as before.

Only now, where its right eye had been, was a hole oozing gore.

Nate barely took that in when the griz was on him. He leaped to try and get out of the way and was caught by a shoulder as hard as a wall. The impact cartwheeled him head over moccasins.

Thudding onto his back, Nate scrambled to regain his feet.

The grizzly turned but instead of attacking it shook its head from side to side.

The wound to its eye, Nate reckoned. Sliding his

tomahawk from under his belt and his Bowie from its sheath, he sprang at his bestial adversary.

He mustn't let the griz run off. He needed to end this once and for all. He swung his tomahawk in an arc, going for the other eye. Short of killing it outright, blinding it would give him an advantage.

But the bear was still shaking its head and the tomahawk missed the eye and glanced off. Blood poured, and the grizzly backed up several steps, blinking furiously

Nate went after it, swinging. He was going for the neck but caught its jaw, eliciting a ferocious growl.

The bear had taken enough.

It lunged, snapping at Nate's arm, and it was short of a miracle that he drew the tomahawk back quickly enough to keep from having his arm bit clean through.

Pivoting, Nate stabbed at its neck. His Bowie went in several inches but then no further as the grizzly twisted away.

And reared once more.

Nate found himself staring up at one of the largest bears he had ever encountered, its razor teeth gleaming, its eyes afire with savagery. The grizzly swooped its head at his and he sidestepped and sank the tomahawk into its neck.

Instinct compelled Nate to skip out of reach and it was well he did. Razor claws flashed past where his face had been.

The grizzly wasn't to be denied. Dropping onto all fours, it came at him like a battering ram. And like a battering ram, it slammed into him so violently, he was flung like a twig in a storm to crash onto the ground with all his senses reeling.

Nate was vaguely aware of someone screaming his name. Of someone else yelling something. He hoped it wasn't the kids. He hoped they had done as he told them. If not....

A shadow fell across him.

Nate rolled and a paw thumped the spot where he had been. He kept rolling as teeth gnashed and snapped missing by mere whiskers. Luck. Pure luck. But no one's luck lasted forever and he cried out when the bear's fangs ripped into his hip. He thought his end had come but he was able to keep rolling and when he felt he was in the clear he stopped and pushed up into a squat.

The grizzly was six feet away with a flap of buckskin and not a little real skin dangling from its mouth.

Nate looked down.

He was missing a patch of leggin four inches across, and blood was welling. It wasn't crippling or mortal but it stung like the dickens.

The grizzly spat out the buckskin.

Nate heaved upright. Both his tomahawk and his Bowie dripped blood. Crouching, he circled, surprised the grizzly didn't close again. Perhaps the wounds he'd inflicted were giving it pause.

Not for long.

With a roar that echoed off the mountains, the grizzly sprang. As quick as it was, Nate was quicker. Avoiding its mashing teeth, he brought the tomahawk down with all his might on an exposed ear even as he drove his Bowie into its neck.

A foreleg flashed and Nate felt searing pain across

his chest.

Then he was on the ground. Again. Flat on his back with scarlet furrows along his ribs.

To lie there was to invite death.

Scrabbling onto his side, he levered erect and braced for the inevitable.

The grizzly was leaving.

Nate couldn't credit his eyes.

The bear was loping toward the forest to the south. As it ran it shook its head, as before. On reaching the tree line it stopped and looked back. Its head and neck were splotched red. The ruined eye still oozed.

"Fight me, damn you!" Nate cried.

The grizzly melted into the vegetation.

Nate took a step to give chase only to have a wave of dizziness bring him to a stop. He was bleeding from his chest and thigh but not a lot.

Small hands plucked at his buckskins.

"You did it!" Clara exclaimed. "You drove it off!"

Behind her Gunther scowled. "He should have killed it."

"He tried," Clara said.

A bigger hand fell on Nate's arm.

"We saw the whole thing!" Charles declared. "I wanted to help but didn't have a clear shot."

"You saved us, Mr. King!" Elizabeth said. "The bear will leave us alone, as hurt as it is. We're safe at last!"

"No," Nate said grimly. "We're not." He started toward where his rifle lay but the dizziness grew worse. His knees buckled and it was all he could do to sit down without collapsing.

Charles bent to steady him. "How bad is it? What

can we do to help?"

"If we had water we could wash his wounds," Elizabeth said.

Nate closed his eyes and took deep breaths. He attributed his condition to the tumbles he took. That last one, he had hit his head so that it rang.

"Want us to go look for water?" Elizabeth said.

"And run into the bear?" Charles said.

"My guns," Nate said.

"What about them?" Charles said.

"Bring them to me." Nate thought to add a, "Please."

Reloading proved a trial.

Nate moved as slow as proverbial molasses. Charles offered to do it for him but Nate told him to keep watch. The settler meant well but the only person Nate trusted with his weapons was himself. Well, and Winona. And Zach. And Evelyn. He grin lopsidedly.

"What can possibly amuse you at a time like this?" Elizabeth said.

"No sign of our tormentor," Charles informed him. "As soon as you're able we'll push on."

"No," Nate said.

"Why on earth not?"

"You and others will keep going."

"What will you be.....?" Charles began, and insight dawned. "Surely not."

"One of us has to."

"Why not the two of us together?"

"Do you really need to ask?"

"Damnation," Charles said.

Chapter 33

The forest lay quiet under the bright afternoon sun. Ominously so. Not a single bird warbled. Nowhere could be seen a scampering squirrel.

Legions of tall trees cast dark shadows that dappled the greenery of the understory and made it difficult for questing eyes to discern movement.

Nate was wariness incarnate. No one knew better than he the fierce nature of his formidable quarry. He had earned his other name---Grizzly Killer---the hard way.

Grizzlies were mountains of muscle and brawn. Their teeth could crush bone. Their claws could rake a man to his innards. Their senses were incredibly sharp, their sense of small sharpest of all. It was said they could smell blood from a mile away. Said, also, that they could smell fear from almost as far.

Nate gave no thought to anything but the hunt. To think of fear was to let it loose. To dwell on it was to shrivel a person's soul to where they were afraid to take a breath.

Nate learned long ago that when in a fight for his life, when pitted against an adversary whether bestial or human, the thing to do was to concentrate on the needs of each and every moment.

Right now his need was to find the bear.

His Hawken was in his hands. His pistols were wedged on either side of his belt buckle. His tomahawk was tucked tight at his side. His Bowie was in its sheath on his other hip.

He placed each moccasin-clad foot with the utmost care. He avoided dry leaves. Avoided, too, twigs that might snap and give him away.

He moved as a stalking cougar---if the cougar was over six feet in height and packed with over two hundred pounds of hard sinew.

The tiniest of motion drew Nate's instant attention.

A butterfly fluttered across a shaft of sunlight and disappeared behind a blue spruce.

A silent sparrow darted from pine to pine.

Nate was sure the grizzly was nearby. He could feel it, as the saying went, in his bones.

He had hurt it, hurt it badly, and it would want to do the same to him.

Grizzlies could be as vengeful as humans.

Fallen pine needles cushioned Nate's stealthy tread as he glided past a spruce. Crouching, he scanned the tangle of vegetation.

The heavy thickets could hide a host of grizzlies.

Nate tested the breeze. His nose was nowhere near the equal of a bear's but if it were close enough, he might detect its musky odor.

He did.

Nate became living stone. Only his eyes moved, darting back and forth, seeking a telltale hint of where the bear lurked.

It could be ten feet away and he wouldn't know it.

Time passed.

STALKED

The odor faded.

Nate stalked to his left to go around a thicket. He was abreast of it when he saw crushed grass. A bit further on, plainly etched in a patch of bare dirt, was the outline of a giant paw.

All Nate asked was for a clear shot.

Just one clear shot at the grizzly's vitals and this would be over and he could get on with his life.

He hoped that Charles and Elizabeth had done as he'd told them and taken Clara and Gunther on down the mountain. If not, the bear might circle around him to get at them.

Nate put a stop to his distracting thoughts. Keep in the moment, he told himself. Watch for the griz and nothing else.

The ground sloped. The vegetation thinned and was replaced by large boulders, singly and in clusters.

Nate debated climbing one for a look-see. He decided against it. He would have to lower his rifle to climb, giving the bear several seconds advantage should it attack.

The layer of pine needles and leaves gave way to patches of gravel.

Nate slowed even more.

The small rocks had a tendency to crunch slightly underfoot. He placed his moccasins as lightly as if he were walking on eggshells.

He was in among the boulders when a sound drew him up short. Not from the boulders, from behind him. It was the merest suggestion of the scrape of a padded paw.

Whirling, Nate crouched, the Hawken to his

shoulder, his trigger finger tensed to squeeze. He wouldn't put it past the grizzly to have let him go by and then come up on him from the rear.

Meat-eaters preferred to take their prey by surprise when they could.

Breathless with expectation, Nate waited. The sound wasn't repeated. In the unnerving quiet he retraced his steps until he was out of the boulders.

Ahead rose the wall of forest.

Again Nate felt unseen eyes on him. It might be his nerves playing tricks but he had learned to trust his instincts. Time and again they had saved his hide from an untimely end.

Keeping low, Nate glided into the trees. He caught a whiff of musky bear odor and knew he was close.

That such a huge creature could hide so well was unsettling.

Nate ventured deeper.

Birds and small animals were still absent. They knew a hulking terror was abroad and were lying low.

He wondered what the grizzly was waiting for.

Then again, the bear would be more cautious now that it was wounded.

Remembering those wounds brought another grim smile.

For all their immense size and frightening ferocity, grizzlies could be hurt. They could be killed.

Nate wasn't leaving the foothills until this particular griz was as dead as dead could be.

A fly buzzed past, its hum unnaturally loud in the awful stillness.

Far off a raven squawked.

The strain of staying constantly alert was beginning to tell. So was the strain on his body. He was like a rope stretched taut.

Nate reached a point where the trees were highest, the shadows darkest.

Barely audible, something wheezed.

Nate swung right, his cheek to his Hawken. He saw nothing. He swung left. Again he saw nothing and went to face around when his brain belatedly registered a pattern in the foliage that wasn't readily apparent. He swung left again and this time a great triangle of dark shadow stood out against the backdrop of green and brown.

It was the grizzly's head.

Needing to be sure of his shot and not have it deflected, Nate took a step nearer. The instant he moved, so did the vegetation, exploding toward him as if blasted by a keg of black powder. Only this explosion was caused by an ursine behemoth that swept toward Nate in a blur.

Nate fired. He didn't want to. He only had a head shot and the grizzly's skull had already proven proof against his lead. Except for its eye. He went for the other eye but he struck the bear's brow, as before.

At that close of range the .60-caliber slowed it.

In those precious seconds Nate bounded aside.

The grizzly swept past, a paw flailing at Nate's chest and missing by a hair's width. Letting go of his Hawken, Nate drew both pistols.

The grizzly was already turning.

He fired into its side, going for the heart. He had no idea if he scored. Even if he had, he knew of an instance where a heart-shot grizzly ran for half a mile before collapsing. Another time, a griz surprised four hunters and one of them shot it in the heart but it still killed two of them before lead to the brainpan brought it down.

Nate fired his second pistol. He aimed for the lungs. Again, whether he hit was impossible to say.

Now all three of his guns were empty.

And the bear was still alive.

Nate unlimbered his tomahawk and unsheathed his Bowie. His aching chest and thigh reminded him that the grizzly's teeth and claws were more than a match for his weapons. He must stay out of its reach while striving to inflict a mortal wound.

Easier contemplated than done.

With a roar that seemed to shake the very ground, the grizzly was on him.

Nate buried his tomahawk in its head, or tried to. The keen edge wasn't keen enough. It glanced off the monster's skull. Glistening teeth sheared at Nate's forearm and snagged his sleeve. He sought to pull lose but the buckskin was caught on a fang.

The grizzly did it for him by cuffing him across the chest, the blow so powerful that the buckskin tore free.

Nate felt as if his ribs had caved in. He wound up on his back awash in agony. A gaping maw filled his vision and he sought to roll aside only to receive another cuff, this time to his shoulder. He was sent crashing into the base of an oak.

Nate still had his tomahawk and his Bowie but he was in a bad way. His mind reeled on the brink of consciousness. A giant hairy leg appeared next to his face and he buried his tomahawk in it. Jaws snapped, closing on the tomahawk and ripping the weapon from his grasp. He speared his Bowie up, seeking the bear's belly. The long blade sheered through fat and muscle, and he felt an intense elation. It was short-lived.

Teeth sank into his shoulder and he was dragged.

In desperation Nate thrust and cut but the grizzly showed no more reaction than if he were tickling it with a feather. Craning his head, he saw its neck. He pushed up, levering with his feet, and speared his Bowie in to the hilt. Blood spurted, covering his fingers. The bear continued to drag him. He dug in his heels and clawed at the earth with his free hand but the grizzly was much too strong.

It went on dragging him.

He bumped over a log, wincing as his knee flared with agony. Then bright sunlight hit his face and he squinted against the harsh glare. His shoulder was released.

Only so the grizzly could bite his side. He had visions of being torn to bits and devoured.

His awareness flickered in and out.

Suddenly the grizzly's face was above his. Its terrifying maw gaped wide.

Nate braced for the sensation of having his head crushed. Then something long and metallic was pressed against the grizzly's ear and a blast blistered Nate's own.

He pitched into nothingness.

Chapter 34

Nate came around slowly. First he was conscious of being conscious.

Next he was aware that he was on his back. His sense of his own body returned, and with it, a rush of pain that made him grit his teeth to keep from crying out.

He hurt all over. It felt as if a tree had fallen on him. Only a few times in his life had he ever hurt this much.

His hands were crossed on his chest. He moved his fingers to see if he could.

"You're awake," said the voice of the person he loved most in all the world.

Nate opened his eyes. It was night. A campfire had burned low. On the other side of it lay forms curled in slumber.

A blanket covered him to his chin.

"Husband," Winona said. She was beside him, her knees tucked to her chest, her eyes alight with happiness.

Nate tried to speak but his mouth was so dry, all he could do was croak.

"Give him this," said someone else in the Ute tongue, and an arm extended toward her with their own water skin.

Sapariche was seated cross-legged by Nate's ankles.

He beamed. "My heart is glad you are among the living again, Grizzly Killer."

Winona opened the water skin and tilted it so Nate could take as many sips as he wanted. "It is about two in the morning," she let him know. "Everyone else is asleep."

Nate swallowed, relishing the taste and the relief for his dry throat. When had had drank enough he looked at her and said simply, "Wife."

They stared into each other's eyes.

Winona broke the spell with, "The Gordon's and Gunther turned in early but Bright Rainbow went to sleep only a little while ago. She was quite worried about you."

"Charles and the others?"

Winona gazed at the sleeping forms. "They are well, all things considered. We ran into them when we were coming to find you. I came on ahead and got here just as the grizzly was about to finish you off."

"That was you who shot it in the head?" Nate realized. Smiling, he reached over and placed his hand on hers.

"I am fond of your own handsome head and would like for it to stay on your shoulders."

Sapariche said, "You might like to know I skinned the bear for you. The hide will make a fine robe."

"Keep it," Nate said.

"Eh?"

"It's yours."

"That would not be right."

"A gift," Nate said. "From one friend to another."

"I thank you, Grizzly Killer." Sapariche was

touched. "It will keep me warm through the winters I have left."

"Are you hungry?" Winona asked.

Nate was mildly surprised to find he wasn't. "I just want to lie here."

"Good," Winona said. "Because I'm not letting you up for at least three days."

"Whatever you want."

Winona grinned. "Oh my. You should be torn up by grizzlies more often."

Nate grunted. If he had a say, he'd never tangle with another bear as long as he lived.

"Once you are fit enough we will go on to Bent's," Winona said. "Charles and Elizabeth are heading back East. They gave Gunther the choice of going to live with his uncle or staying with them."

"He chose them," Nate guessed.

Winona nodded. "That's not all. It is a good thing we married when we did."

Now it was Nate who said, "Eh?"

"Clara told her mother that she thinks you are the bravest man who ever lived and if she were old enough, she would marry you."

"She didn't."

Winona grinned. "What is it about you that girls and bears like you so much?"

"I'm just lucky I guess," Nate King said.

FINI

Be on the lookout for more great reads by David Robbins!

A GIRL, THE END OF THE WORLD AND EVERYTHING

Courtney Hewitt lived a perfectly ordinary life. Then several countries let fly with nuclear missiles and chemical and biological weapons and her life was no longer ordinary. Now Courtney has chemical clouds and radiation to deal with. To say nothing of the not-so-dead who eat the living.

A GIRL A DOG AND ZOMBIES ON THE MUNCH

Courtney Hewitt is having a bad week. First World War III broke out. Then she lost contact with her family. Toxic chemical clouds appeared. So did dead people who crave to eat the living. As well as horrible mutations, bloodthirsty gangs, and outright crazies. On the plus side she found a dog.

ENDWORLD DOOMSDAY

Armageddon! World War III! At a remote site in Minnesota, filmmaker Kurt Carpenter has built a secure compound and invited a select group to join him until the worst is over. They think they are prepared for anything. They're wrong.

ANGEL U
LET THERE BE LIGHT

Armageddon is a generation away. The forces of light and darkness will clash in the ultimate battle. To prepare humankind, the angels establish a university of literal higher learning here on Earth. Enroll now---before the demons get you.

ANGEL U
DEMIGOD

Gilgamesh the Destroyer. Demon-slayer. Son of the Moon. Two parts god, one part human. He wants nothing to do with the war between Heaven and Hell. Then Gilgamesh learns that he is not who he thought he was. He is not *what* he thought he was. To learn the truth, Gilgamesh will venture where few have dared.

ENDWORLD #28
DARK DAYS

The science fiction series that sweeps its readers into a terrifying Apocalyptic future. The Warriors of Alpha Triad face their greatest threat. Their survivalist compound, the Home, has been invaded. Not by an enemy army. This time a shapeshifter is loose among the Family. Able to change into anyone at will, it is killing like there is no tomorrow.

ENDWORLD #29
THE LORDS OF KISMET

From out of the horror of World War III, a new menace is spawned, Claiming to be the gods of old, their goal is global conquest. Three Warriors are sent to bring the Lords down---but there is more to the creatures than anyone imagined.

ENDWORLD #30
SYNTHEZOIDS

The survivors of the Apocalypse have endured a lot. Mutations. Chemical toxins. Madmen. Now a new threat arises---living horrors, thanks to science gone amok.

BLOOD FEUD #2
HOUNDS OF HATE

Chace and Cassie Shannon are back. The feud between the Harkeys and the Shannons takes the twins from the hills of Arkansas to New Orleans, where Chace has a grand scheme to set them up in style. But if the Harkeys have anything to say about it, they'll be ripped to pieces.

THE WERELING

The original Horror classic. Ocean City has a lot going for it. Nice beaches. The boardwalk. Tourists. But something new is prowling Ocean City. Something that feasts on those tourists. Something that howls at the moon, and bullets can't stop. The Jersey Shore werewolf is loose.

HIT RADIO

Franco Scarvetti has a problem. His psycho son has whacked a made man. Now a rival Family is out to do the same to his son. So Big Frank comes up with a plan. He sends his lethal pride and joy to run a radio station in a small town while he tries to smooth things over. But Big Frank never read Shakespeare and he forgets that a psycho by any other name is still....a psycho.

WILDERNESS #67
THE GIFT

Evelyn King is sixteen and in love. She tricks her father and sneaks away with the warrior she loves---straight into a pack of killers.

WILDERNESS #68
SAVAGE HEARTS

Nate and Winona King thought they were doing the right thing when they rode deep into the Rockies to return a little girl to her people. But some good deeds are fraught with perils.

WILDERNESS #69
THE AVENGER

From out of the past comes a threat the King family never expects. A killer who wants an eye for an eye. His quarry? Zach King, son of Grizzly Killer.

WILDERNESS #70
LOVE AND COLD STEEL

The heart wants what the heart wants. But what if your heart leads you and the one you love into danger? Evelyn King is set to marry the man of her dreams. If they live long enough.

Made in United States
Troutdale, OR
03/18/2024